P9-DWG-608

D0037815

SPENCE + LILA

The Harper Short Novel Series

By the same author

IN COUNTRY

SHILOH AND OTHER STORIES

BOBBIE ANN MASON

SPENCE + LILA

ILLUSTRATIONS BY LaNELLE MASON

1817

HARPER & ROW, PUBLISHERS, New York

Cambridge, Philadelphia, San Francisco, Washington
London, Mexico City, São Paulo, Singapore, Sydney

SPENCE + LILA. Copyright © 1988 by Bobbie Ann Mason. All rights reserved. Printed in the United States of America. No part of this book may be used or reproduced in any manner whatsoever without written permission except in the case of brief quotations embodied in critical articles and reviews. For information address Harper & Row, Publishers, Inc., 10 E. 53rd Street, New York, N.Y. 10022. Published simultaneously in Canada by Fitzhenry & Whiteside Ltd., Toronto.

FIRST EDITION

Copyeditor: *Marjorie Horvitz*

Designer: *Lydia Link*

Library of Congress Cataloging-in-Publication Data

Mason, Bobbie Ann.
  Spence + Lila.

  (The Harper short novel series)
  I. Title. II. Title: Spence and Lila.
PS3563.A7877S64   1988   813'.54   87-46155
ISBN 0-06-015911-1

---

88 89 90 91 92 MPC 10 9 8 7 6 5 4 3

For my parents
and for Janice, LaNelle, Don, and Roger

SPENCE + LILA

*O*N THE WAY to the hospital in Paducah, Spence notices the row of signs along the highway: WHERE WILL YOU BE IN ETERNITY? Each word is on a white cross. The message reminds him of the old Burma-Shave signs. His wife, Lila, beside him, has been quiet during the trip, which takes forty minutes in his Rabbit. He didn't take her car because it has a hole in the muffler, but she has complained about his car ever since he cut the seat belts off to deactivate the annoying warning buzzer.

As they pass the Lone Oak shopping center, on the outskirts of Paducah, Lila says fretfully, "I don't know if the girls will get here."

"They're supposed to be here by night," Spence reminds her. Ahead, a gas station marquee advertises a free case of Coke with a tune-up.

Catherine, their younger daughter, has gone to pick up Nancy at the airport in Nashville. Although Lila objected to the trouble and expense, Nancy is flying all the way from Boston. Cat lives nearby, and Nancy will stay with her. Nancy offered to stay with Spence, so he wouldn't be alone, but he insisted he would be all right.

When Cat brought Lila home from the doctor the day before and Lila said, "They think it's cancer," the words ran through him like electricity. She didn't cry all evening, and when he tried to hold her, he couldn't speak. They sat in the living room in their recliner chairs, silent and scared,

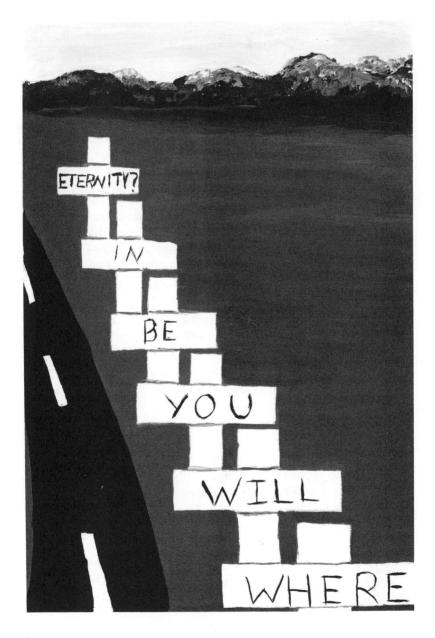

watching TV just as they usually did. Before she sat down for the evening, she worked busily in the kitchen, freezing vegetables from the garden and cooking food for him to eat during her stay in the hospital. He couldn't eat any supper except a bowl of cereal, and she picked at some ham and green beans.

He knew she had not been feeling well for months; she'd had dizzy spells and she had lost weight. The doctor at the local clinic told her to come back in three months if she kept losing weight, but Cat insisted on taking her mother to Paducah. The doctors were better there, Cat insisted, in that know-it-all manner both his daughters had. Cat, who was careless with money, didn't even think to ask what the specialists would charge. When she brought Lila home, it was late—feeding time. Spence was at the pond feeding the ducks, with Oscar, the dog. When Oscar saw the car turn into the driveway, he tore through the soybean field toward the house, as if he, too, were anxious for a verdict.

They had told Lila that her dizzy spells were tiny strokes. They also found a knot in her right breast. They wanted to take the knot out and do a test on it, and if it was cancer they would take her whole breast off, right then. It was an emergency, Lila explained. They couldn't deal with the strokes until they got the knot out. Spence imagined the knot growing so fast it would eat her breast up if she waited another day or two.

They're crawling through the traffic on the edge of Paducah. When he was younger, Spence used to come and watch the barges on the river. They glided by confidently, like miniature flattops putting out to sea. He has wanted to take Lila for a cruise on the *Delta Queen,* the luxury steamboat that paddles all the way to New Orleans, but he hasn't been able to bring himself to do it.

He turns on the radio and a Rod Stewart song blares out.

"Turn that thing off!" Lila yells.

"I thought you needed a little entertainment," he says, turning the sound down.

She rummages in her purse for a cigarette, her third on the trip. "They won't let me have any cigarettes tonight, so I better smoke while I got a chance."

"I'll take them things and throw 'em away," he says.

"You better not."

She cracks the window open at the top to let the smoke out. Her face is the color of cigarette ashes. She looks bad.

"I guess it's really cancer," she says, blowing out smoke. "The X-ray man said it was cancer."

"How would he know? He ain't even a doctor."

"He's seen so many, he would know."

"He ain't paid to draw that conclusion," Spence says. "Why did he want to scare you like that? Didn't the doctor say he'd have to wait till they take the knot out and look at it?"

"Yeah, but—" She fidgets with her purse, wadding her cigarette package back into one of the zipper pockets. "The X-ray man sees those X-rays all day long. He knows more about X-rays than a doctor does."

Spence turns into the hospital parking lot, unsure where to go. The eight-story hospital cuts through the humid, hazy sky, like a stray sprig of milo growing up in a bean field. A car pulls out in front of him. Spence's reactions are slow today, but he hits the brakes in time.

"I think I'll feel safer in the hospital," Lila says.

Walking from the parking lot, he carries the small bag she packed. He suspects there is a carton of cigarettes in it. Cat keeps trying to get Lila to quit, but Lila has no willpower. Once Cat gave her a cassette tape on how to quit smoking, but Lila accidentally ran it through the washing machine. It was in a shirt pocket. "Accidentally on purpose," Cat accused her. Cat even told Lila once that cigarettes caused breast cancer. But Spence believes worry causes it. She worries about Cat, the way she has been running around with men she hardly knows since her divorce last year. It's a bad example for her two small children, and Lila is afraid the men aren't serious about Cat. Lila keeps saying no one will want to marry a woman with two extra mouths to feed.

Now Lila says, "I want you to supervise that garden. The girls won't know how to take care of it. That corn needs to be froze, and the beans are still coming in."

"Don't worry about your old garden," he says impatiently. "Maybe I'll mow it down."

"Spence!" Lila cries, grabbing his arm tightly. "Don't you go and mow down my garden!"

"You work too hard on it," he says. "We don't need all that grub anymore for just us two."

"The beans is about to begin a second round of blooming," she says. "I want to let most of them make into shellies and save some for seed. And I don't want the corn to get too old."

The huge glass doors of the hospital swing open, and a nurse pushes out an old woman in a wheelchair. The woman is bony and pale, with a cluster of kinfolks in bluejeans around her. Her aged hands, folded in her lap, are spotted like little bird dogs. The air-conditioning blasts Spence and Lila as they enter, and he feels as though they are walking into a meat locker.

$\mathcal{S}$ HE FELT that lump weeks ago, but she
didn't mention it then. When she and Spence returned
from a trip to Florida recently, she told Cat about it, and
Cat started pestering her to see a specialist. The knot did
feel unusual, like a piece of gristle. The magazines said
you would know it was different. Lila never examined her
breasts the way they said to do, because her breasts were
always full of lumps anyway—from mastitis, which she
had several times. Her breasts are so enormous she cannot
expect to find a little knot. Spence says her breasts are like
cow bags. He has funny names for them, like the affec-
tionate names he had for his cows when they used to keep
milk cows. Names like Daisy and Bossy. Petunia. Prim-
rose. It will be harder on him if she loses one of her breasts
than it will be on her. Women can stand so much more
than men can.

She makes him leave the hospital early, wanting to be
alone so she can smoke a cigarette in peace. After he
brought her in, he paced around, then went downstairs for
a Coke. Now he leaves to go home, and she watches him
from behind as he trudges down the corridor, hugging
himself in the cold. Lila is glad she brought her housecoat,
but even with it she is afraid she will take pneumonia.

In the lounge, she smokes and plays with a picture
puzzle laid out on a card table. Someone has pieced most
of the red barn and pasture, and a vast blue sky remains

to be done. Lila loves puzzles. When she was little, growing up at her uncle's, she had a puzzle of a lake scene with a castle. She worked that puzzle until the design was almost worn away. The older folks always kidded her, but she kept working the puzzle devotedly. She always loved the satisfying snap of two pieces going together. It was like knowing something for sure.

Her son Lee towers in the doorway of the lounge. She stands up, surprised.

"Did you get off work early?" He works at Ingersoll-Rand.

"No. I just took off an hour, and I have to go back and work till nine. They're working me overtime this month." He has lines on his face and he is only thirty-two.

He hugs her silently. He's so tall her head pokes his armpit, where he has always been ticklish.

"I didn't know you were that sick in Florida," he says. "We shouldn't have dragged you through Disney World."

"I knew something was wrong, but I didn't know what." She explains the details of the X-rays and the operation, then says, "I'm going to lose my breast, Lee."

"You are?" The lines on his face freeze. He needs a shave.

"They won't know till they get in there, but if it's cancer they'll go ahead and take it out."

"Which one?"

"This one," she says, cupping her right breast.

A woman with frizzy red hair hobbles into the lounge, her hospital gown exposing her fat, doughy knees. "I was looking for my husband," she says, "but I reckon he ain't here."

Lila waits for the woman to leave, then laughs. She's still holding her breast. "You don't remember sucking on these, do you, Lee?" She loves to tease her son. "You

sucked me dry and I had to put you on a bottle after two months. I couldn't make enough milk to feed you."

With an embarrassed grin, Lee looks out the window. "I believe you're making that up."

"You want one last tug?" She reaches up and tousles his hair. His eyes are her eyes—the same vacant blue, filled with specks, like markings on a baby bird. They both laugh, and she takes a cigarette from her housecoat pocket. Lee lights it for her, then lights his own cigarette. They share a Coke from a cooler filled with ice and free cold drinks in cans for visitors in the lounge. Lila's proud of her son. He has such a pretty wife and two smart kids, but he has to work too hard to keep up his house and car payments.

"Spence didn't know about these drinks," she says. "He went all the way down to the basement to the machine."

"He didn't stick around five minutes, I bet," Lee says, handing her the can.

"Lord, no. These places give him the heebie-jeebies."

"They do me too." Lee is playing with his lighter, flicking the flame on and off. "When's Nancy coming in?"

"I don't know. Cat called from the airport before we left home and said Nancy's airplane was late. They was supposed to get here by about four o'clock." She sips from the Coke and hands it back to Lee.

"Did Cat take off from work?"

Lila nods. "I told the girls they didn't have to go to all this trouble, but I guess they're scared I'm going to kick the bucket."

"No, you won't," Lee says. He hesitates, trying to say something, but he's exactly like Spence, bashful and silent at all the wrong moments. "What caused this?" he asks. "Do the doctors know what they're doing?"

"They're specialists," Lila says. "The woman that runs the dress store where Cat works recommended the doctor I went to yesterday. He's supposed to be good." Touching her son's knee, she says, "Promise me one thing, Lee."

He flicks ash off his cigarette by tapping it from beneath with his little finger. "What?"

"That you and Cat will start talking to one another. I can't believe my own children would hate each other."

"We don't hate each other!"

"Well, you could be nice to each other—it wouldn't hurt."

Lee stubs out his cigarette in the ashtray and nods his head thoughtfully. "I'll try," he says. "But it's up to her." He stands. "I have to get back to work."

"Are you going home for supper?"

"No. I'll grab a Big Mac or something."

Lee walks her back to her room and gives her another hug. His belt buckle presses under her breasts. When he was about fourteen, he started shooting up like a cornstalk and she thought he'd never stop. He was named after Lila's father, who abandoned her when she was four and went off to Alaska—long before it was a state. Lila was never sure it was appropriate to name her only son after him, but it's Christian to forgive. Now, as he leaves, she suddenly feels the fear she felt when Nancy left home for the first time—certain she won't see her child again.

After experimenting with the remote-control device, Lila watches television for a while. The news doesn't make any sense. The commercials are about digestion. Her digestion has always been good. Spence has heartburn and can't eat much for supper. Sometimes he has chest pains, but he says it's just heartburns. On the news, a couple about her age have won over three million dollars in a lottery. "We'll pay off the bills, I guess," the man says. "And get a new living room suit," the woman adds.

A nurse trots in with some forms for Lila to fill out.

"I can't see good enough," Lila says, searching for her glasses in her purse. "My glasses don't fit anymore, but my daughter says that's what I get for buying them at the dime store." She laughs and holds the forms at arm's length. Pointing to the blurred fine print, she asks, "What's this say?"

"It's just routine, ma'am," says the nurse. "Tonight when the doctor comes he'll give you a release form and read it to you and make sure you understand everything that's going on."

"What's going to happen to me?"

Before the nurse can answer, a girl walks in and plunks down Lila's supper tray without comment.

"My, you're getting a feast tonight," says the nurse, sending the tray toward Lila on a roller platform that fits over the bed. On the tray are dark broth, red Jell-O, black coffee.

"Couldn't I have ice tea?" Lila asks. "Coffee makes me prowl all night."

"Don't worry. We'll give you a sleeping pill."

Lila watches the sports news, something she would never do at home. When the weather comes on, she pays careful attention. The radar map shows rain everywhere in the adjoining states, but none in western Kentucky. They need rain bad. They had too much rain back in the spring. The high today was eighty-nine.

The liquid supper splashes in her stomach. From behind the curtain partition, a woman is groaning. A nurse coaxes her out of bed and helps her walk out of the room. The patient is old, her face distorted with pain as she clutches a pillow to her belly.

Lila hasn't felt so alone since Spence was in the Navy. Nancy was two, and they were still living with Spence's parents. Rosie and Amp were so quiet, their faces set like concrete as they lost themselves in their chores. Lila was awkward in Rosie's kitchen, with Rosie hovering over her. When Lila wanted to warm food for Nancy, Rosie insisted that Lila had to use a certain small aluminum pan, so they wouldn't have to wash a large one. But the food always stuck to the little pan, and it was hard to scrape clean. Rosie washed dishes in an enamel pan set on a gas ring and scalded them in another pan on another ring. The scum of the slippery lye soap never really washed off the dishes. Rosie added the dirty dishwater to the slop bucket for the hogs. Hogs liked the taste, she said. That fall, a neighbor helped Amp butcher a hog and Rosie made lye soap from the fat. Lila sewed sausage casings from flour sacks. She added flecks of dried red peppers to the ground sausage. She added more than she should have, because she knew Spence liked it extra hot, and she wanted it to be spicy for him when he came home. She knew he would come home.

Lila had to talk to somebody, so she chattered away to Nancy in their room. She was still stunned by the new experience of having a baby. Nancy kept on nursing, and Lila let her, even though her teeth made the nipples sore. She read Spence's letters aloud to her. Nancy couldn't understand the words, but Lila knew she needed her daddy, and that was the best Lila could do to help her feel his existence. Nancy listened, serious and focused, like a curious bird. There was not much to see out there, he wrote—a few birds resting on the waves like setting hens, and now and then playful porpoises that seemed to do circus tricks in the water. Spence wrote about a storm at sea, in which the boat rocked like a tire swing, the waves washing the deck. The ship stopped at an island in the Philippines and he got a twelve-hour shore leave. He wrote messages to Nancy—had she learned to milk a cow yet? was she shedding her baby teeth? Silly things, to be funny. Not until he got home did he tell about the deafening noises of the war, a racket like the end of the world.

Their room was unheated and they had a hard winter. Nancy caught cold after cold, and Lila huddled her close in the bed, under the weight of half a dozen quilts. She was afraid of rolling over on her, the way a sow sometimes mashed her pigs. One night Lila woke up and found Nancy uncovered, wet and shivering. After that, the cold went into pneumonia. Lila wanted to take her to the doctor, but Amp protested, "Why, he would charge! We can doctor her." Rosie baked onions in ashes and squeezed the juice into a spoon and fed it to her. At night Lila warmed the bed with heated bricks wrapped in newspaper, and she hardly slept, making sure she kept the child covered up; in the daytime she made a bed for her in a box close to the fireplace. She wrapped her chest in greased rags. One frightening night, when Lila prayed so hard she was almost screaming, Nancy's fever finally broke, and gradually her breathing improved. Over the following weeks, as Nancy grew stronger, Lila kept talking to her, singing and reading Spence's letters aloud, trying to find new meaning and hope in each one. Finally, there was a warm spell, when the north wind didn't blow through the cracks around the windows of their room. The yellow bushes in front of the house put out some blooms, and some geese flew over.

Uneasily, Lila and Rosie sat by the fire and pieced quilt blocks, tuning in the war news on the radio at intervals. Their shared silent worry about Spence gradually drew them together, and eventually Lila loved Spence's parents as though they were her own. That spring, during a fierce electrical storm, they gathered in Amp and Rosie's bedroom and wrapped feather bolsters around themselves. Amp said lightning wouldn't strike feathers. "Did you ever see a chicken get hit by lightning?" Rosie asked.

*　　*　　*

Suddenly Lila's daughters are there, rushing to hug her. They're smiling too much. Nancy's eyes have that deep, private look Lila has often seen in them. She drops her backpack and tote bag on the bed and buries her head on Lila's shoulder. Lila's face is full of Nancy's hair, smelling faintly of shampoo. Nancy always washed her hair too much. Lila was forever warning Nancy not to go outside with a wet head or she would catch cold, but Nancy wouldn't listen, determined to do things her own way.

Cat smells like perfume, maybe the scent of irises. Lila rarely gets hugs from her, even though they are closer in some ways, because she hasn't moved away like Nancy and her comings and goings aren't such big events. Cat came running home in tears when she began having trouble with Dan, but Nancy never mentions anything wrong in her life. Nancy analyzes everything closely, passing judgment on it, the way her grandmother would have examined someone's quilt—studying and evaluating the stitching for evenness and smallness. Nancy would never make a quilt, though. But Cat would.

"My plane got fog-delayed in Boston," Nancy says, pulling back from Lila. "And instead of landing in Nashville, we flew all the way to Birmingham and then back to Nashville. How are you feeling, Mom?"

"Well, I ain't ready to go out and pick cotton," says Lila. "But you didn't have to come all this way."

[27]

"I wanted to come."

Cat says, "I ate lunch twice while I was waiting for the plane. And read two whole magazines from cover to cover. And watched people. I saw a lot of weirdos."

Nancy plops on the side of the bed. "When Cat's nervous she eats, and when I'm nervous I can't eat."

Cat, her car keys still in her hand, has on a long skirt with a flounce, from the boutique where she works. Nancy dresses like a boy most of the time and has worn the same belt on her bluejeans for years, but Cat has always been a fashion plate. In high school she was Miss Sorghum at a festival. Cat used to get exasperated with Nancy and say she didn't want to be seen in public with her, but she's finally given up on her sister. Cat always said, "Be fancy, Nancy!"

The girls run through a million questions they want to ask the doctor, but Lila cannot remember what she wants to ask. She meant to tell the doctor yesterday about her mastitis and to ask whether it causes cancer. The main thing is the cost. Cat assured her everything would be covered, but Lila doesn't believe Medicare covers everything. She heard that if it was cancer, it wouldn't be covered. Now Cat is investigating the drawers and closets in the room, checking things. Cat has always been particular. She's a fine housekeeper, something Lila never had time to be. Cat won dozens of ribbons in 4-H.

"Look what I hatched out," Lila says proudly to the nurse who comes in to take her temperature. "My little girls."

"They don't look a thing alike," the nurse says, then glances at her watch.

After the nurse removes the thermometer and leaves, Nancy says, "Robert wanted me to tell you he misses you and he's sorry he couldn't come."

Lila smiles. Her grandson is a thoughtful boy, always sending her cards on Mother's Day and her birthday.

"Jack too," Nancy says.

"Jack's awful good to let you come traipsing down here."

Nancy flinches in protest. "He didn't *let* me! He had nothing to do with it. You're my mom and I came to see you."

The bed is loaded with Nancy's things, blue pouches with zipper pockets. Lila thrives on such confusion. She teases Nancy, "I swear with all that stuff you tote around you're just like old Aunt Hattie Cross. Aunt Hattie always carried her wash pan and her toothbrush everywhere she went. We kidded her about packing her potty around. We'd say she brushed her teeth in her pot."

"I've got my toothbrush right here—somewhere," Nancy says, grinning. "I didn't bring my pot, though."

"Well, you can use mine," Lila says with a laugh. "There's one in the bathroom with my name on it!"

She tousles Nancy's hair lovingly. Lila's children are all grown, with their own families. This is what life comes down to, she realizes—replacing your own life with new ones. It's just like raising a crop. Somehow, this makes her think of prize-winning vegetables at the fair. It always made her sad to see the largest and prettiest vegetables on display. The best tomatoes and corn and broccoli sat there and ruined just so people could look at them.

"Lee was here," Lila says. "He said he'd talk to you, Cat, but it was up to you. I wish y'all would stop fussing over that air conditioner."

"It wasn't the air conditioner. It was that dumb three-wheeler!" Cat says angrily. "He never should have let Scott ride it. He was too little, and he didn't have a helmet. Those things are dangerous!"

"Where are Scott and Krystal?" Lila asks, shifting the subject.

"With Dan. They went to Hopkinsville yesterday to stay two weeks with him. I thought you knew that."

"No." Lila is puzzled. She says, "I can't keep things straight anymore. I thought Lee was mad at you over that air conditioner you gave him. I didn't know it was the three-wheeler."

Cat pats Lila's hair. "Let's don't worry about this stuff, O.K.?"

Nancy says, "The main thing right now is you."

"I think they're going to take this breast off," Lila says, placing her hand under her right breast.

"You've always been so proud of those," Cat says, reaching to touch the top of Lila's breast lightly.

"My big jugs," Lila says, smiling. "I raised three younguns on these. I guess they're give out now." She can't say what she feels—that the last thing she would have expected was to be attacked by disease in the very place she felt strongest. It seemed to suggest some basic failing, like the rotten core of a dying tree.

Nancy rests her hand on her mother's shoulder. "Is all this too fast?" she asks.

"Well, I have to get it done."

"It's up to you—if you feel it's going too far, or if you want to wait." Nancy removes her hand to smooth her hair. Lila spots a gray hair on Nancy's head and almost bursts into tears.

"No, I want to get it over with."

"We hate to see you pushed around," Cat says. "They're your breasts, and if they're worth more to you than all this—"

"It's your decision," says Nancy.

"I know what you mean," says Lila, cradling her breasts like babies. "But they ain't worth more than living."

"I think it's going to be all right, Mom," says Nancy, taking Lila's hand. "The lump isn't big and you found it early."

"I wouldn't have found it if it hadn't been for Cat." Lila starts to cry. "Don't y'all stare at me. I don't like to be stared at."

The old woman in the other bed, behind a curtain, yells at a nurse, "You can just take that thing and ram it up your butt."

Cat and Nancy start snickering. "I'll be like that tomorrow!" says Lila, laughing back her tears. "Oh, me!"

THREE

$\mathcal{S}$PENCE can't sleep. With the frenzied urgency of a hunting dog, Oscar is barking at an animal out in the field. Spence wonders if it could be the wildcat that had screamed out by the barn one night. Wildcats scavenged at the dump beyond the industrial park, and a man had shot one there not long ago. Spence was heartsick when he heard about that. Some people would shoot anything, just to see how it killed. Last year, he saw, for perhaps ten seconds, a wildcat at the pond. It was small and scrawny, with a short, black-tipped tail and long, tufted ears. It disappeared into the scrub along the creek.

He jams pillows under his neck. They are soft like her breasts, but he doesn't want to let himself think about her body. She has been looking bad for a long time, losing weight, not eating. She kept making excuses, saying she wasn't hungry, or that she was more active than usual. In early June, when they were in Florida, she was sick. They went with Lee and his wife, Joy, and the kids, all crammed in Lee's station wagon. It was the wrong season. When Lee planned the trip, they didn't think about the season because they could only go in the summer, after Joy finished the school year. She teaches the second grade. In Florida, the temperature was already in the high nineties. They stayed in a cabin at Flamingo, the southernmost point on the U.S. mainland. When they entered the cabin, clouds of mosquitoes swarmed in through the door with them.

Afterward, they laughed at the way they had frantically slapped at the insects and sprayed each other down with insect repellent. It reminded Spence of spraying cows for flies. After they wiped out the mosquito invasion, he and Lee sat in the air-conditioning and watched TV while Lila and Joy cooked supper. The children, Jennifer and Greg, scratched their bites until they were raw. Through the night mosquitoes whined only occasionally, and then the next day the hot sun burned them off. Spence loved the heat. As they rode along the main highway, he told Lila, "I wouldn't mind having a job mowing the shoulders along the road down here."

It was his first real trip since he was in the Navy. He was surprised at how much he loved the swamp. On a lookout point, they gazed out over the endless sea of saw grass. It was studded with little rises, like islands. The Indians called them hummocks. He felt free. The sun blazed down on them, and he thought he could live there always. Lee kept apologizing for bringing them to Florida in the wrong season. Most of the migrating birds had gone north. In the winter, thousands of herons and egrets and storks and ibises gathered in the Everglades, but in the late spring the swamp was bare, with only a few birds, and the alligator hole was quiet, the alligators lying still like rotting logs in the murky water. Once, they spotted an alligator crossing the road, sluggish and lizard-like. They saw a blue racer. And several long-necked white birds. A few blue herons.

Lila didn't like Florida. Earlier in the trip, when she started having the dizzy spells and the numbness in her arm, they took her to a hospital in Orlando. The doctor—who charged sixty-five dollars for an emergency-room visit and spent only five minutes with Lila—said she had an irritated nerve and suggested she go to her own doctor when she returned home. They spent two miserable days at Disney World—the purpose of the whole trip, for the kids. Spence didn't care for it. He wanted to see snakes and birds and alligators, so Lee drove them on down to the Everglades. They had insisted Lila didn't have to go, but she said she didn't mind, that she felt better. But when they explored the trails, she stayed in the car, with the air conditioner blowing, and smoked and napped, while Spence and the others explored the boardwalk trails through the swamps. He was fascinated by the mahogany hummocks, and he read all the plaques that told about the wildlife. He liked to imagine when the Indians lived there in the swamp, venturing from hummock to hummock in their canoes, exploring. Back in the stuffy, smoky car, she was quiet and her face was pale, but she said she was all right. "It's the heat," she said. "I'm hotter than a she-wolf in a pepper patch!"

Those dizzy spells turned out to be little strokes— TIAs, the doctor in Paducah called them. The blood wasn't feeding to her brain. Now Spence shudders in the night, imagining a scene in Florida—Lila having a major stroke on one of those lonely trails. The nearest hospital was fifty miles away, and they would not have known how to find it. If something had happened to her then, he would have been to blame.

Dawn is creeping under the shades. The sheets are wadded, the quilt is lying on the rug, the cat scratching at the back door. Lila is crazy about the cat, Abraham. Spence has never seen her so crazy about a cat, the way she baby-talks to him. The morning after Spence heard that wildcat, Abraham's fur was ruffled, as though something had been chewing on him and rolling him in the dirt. Abraham has long hair and is spotted like a Guernsey. Stiff and aching, Spence gets up and watches the sun rise over the soybean fields. Oscar is out there, walking slowly, sniffing close to the ground.

While CNN blares out the latest on Iran-Iraq, Iran-contra, Nicaragua, South Africa, something in Idaho, Spence makes breakfast in the microwave. He watches the strips of bacon curl up and ooze grease down the ridges of the bacon rack. When the bacon is done, he makes scrambled eggs. He sets the dish in for twenty-five seconds, then stirs the eggs with a fork and cooks them for twenty-five more seconds. Spence bought the microwave so he could fix his meals while Lila was away on her trips with the senior citizens. She has been to Hawaii, the Badlands, Savannah and New Orleans.

He bought the microwave at a flea market, almost new. At first, he set it on top of the refrigerator, but Lila couldn't reach it. So he found a wobbly metal table at a sale and set the oven on it next to the kitchen table. The first time he tried the microwave, he cracked an egg in a dish and the egg exploded in the oven with a sound like a shotgun. He learned to punch the yolk with a fork to let the pressure out. "Crazy thing," Lila said on the telephone to one of her friends. "He never reads the directions to anything." The oven came with an incomplete set of instructions, and he had to learn how to use it by trial and error. Once, he exploded a potato, for fun.

After eating, he and Oscar head for the barn to feed the calves, five little Holsteins he is raising for beef in a pasture between the barn and the woods. The fencing is makeshift—boards and an electric wire.

"Oscar, you sure are smart," Spence says. "You learned about that electric fence in one easy lesson."

Oscar wags his tail. The calves flick flies with their tails. They amble forward, rubbing each other and gazing at Spence with liquid eyes the texture and size of fried

eggs. A horrifying image flashes through his mind—jabbing their eyes with a fork. Once he tried raising a veal calf, and every time he remembers it he hates himself. The little thing stayed in the dark stall alone, and whenever Spence came to bottle-feed him, the calf cried. When after only a few weeks Spence took him to the slaughterhouse, the calf couldn't stand up. The meat was tender and pale. He and Lila couldn't talk about it. The packages languished in the freezer, and by the time she cooked the last ones, the meat had lost its freshness.

He steadies himself against the barn door for a moment, then enters the barn, the calves following. He distributes cups of feed into the troughs, and the calves dig their heads in. He fastens their necks to the stanchions, and while they feed he talks to them.

"Sunflower," he says. "You're too skinny. Whoa, there, Mudpuddle. Watch what you're doing, Dexter. Delbert. Boss Hogg, don't get crazy now."

Always, when Spence feeds his calves, he goes through their names.

FOUR

$\mathcal{L}$ ILA SAYS, "They sure don't let you get lonesome here—all the traipsing in and out they do at all hours."

Cat and Nancy are hovering over the bed, staring at her with an unnatural sort of eagerness. "Did you sleep?" Cat asks.

"Off and on," says Lila. She tries to sit up against the pillow, but she feels woozy from this morning's medicine. "That coffee last night made me jumpy, but they give me some pills and a shot."

Nancy says, "That's outrageous! There was no good reason to give you coffee. You should have refused it."

Cat's earrings dangle in Lila's face. Lila's mind feels fuzzy, far away. She is afraid the operating room will be cold.

"Are you scared?" Nancy asks, holding Lila's hand.

"They work you over too much for you to be scared. I haven't had time to think." Lila squeezes Nancy's hand and reaches for Cat's. "You girls are being good to me," she says. "I sure am lucky."

"Well, we care about you," Cat says.

"You're going to be just fine, Mom," says Nancy. "You're tough."

"I guess I better say goodbye to my jug," Lila says, laughing and looking down at herself. "If Spence don't hurry on here, he's going to miss his chance."

Just then Spence appears, still in short sleeves. Yesterday she tried to tell him to wear long sleeves, but he wouldn't listen to her. After giving Nancy a hug, he steps back and eyes her up and down to see how much older she seems.

"You look poor as a snake," he says. "Why didn't you bring Robert?"

"He's going off to camp tomorrow. Jack's taking him up to New Hampshire. It's the same place he went last year, where they go on treks into the mountains."

"Bring him down here. I'll see that he communes with nature." Spence grins at Nancy.

"I'm sure you will. You'll have him out planting soybeans." Nancy twists out of a nurse's way.

"It would be good for him," Lila says sleepily. "Working out in the fields would teach him something."

She closes her eyes, vaguely listening to Spence and the girls talk. If this is her time to go, she should be ready. And she has her family with her, except for Lee, who had to work. She feels she is looking over her whole life, holding it up to see how it has turned out—like a piece of sewing. She can see Cat trying on a dress Lila has made for her, and Lila checks to see whether it needs taking up. She turns up the hem, jerks the top to see how it fits across the shoulders, considers an extra tuck in the waist. In a recurrent dream she has had for years, she is trying to finish a garment, sewing fast against the clock.

They are still chattering nervously around her when the surgeon appears. He's young, with sensitive hands that look skilled at delicate finger work. Lila always notices people's fingers. Nancy and Cat keep asking questions, but Lila is sleepy and can't follow all that he is saying. Then he moves closer to her and says, "If the biopsy shows a malignancy, I'm going to recommend a modified radical mastectomy. I'll remove the breast tissue and the lymph nodes under the arm. But I'll leave the chest muscles. If you follow the physical therapy, then you'll have full use of your arm and you'll be just fine." He smiles reassuringly. He resembles a cousin of Lila's— Whip Stanton, a little man with a lisp and a wife with palsy.

"How small would the lump have to be for you to recommend a lumpectomy instead?" Nancy asks the doctor.

"Infinitesimal," he says. "It's better to get it all out and be sure. This way is more certain."

"Well, more and more doctors are recommending lumpectomies instead of mastectomies," Nancy argues. "What I'm asking is, what is the dividing line? How large should the lump be for the mastectomy to be preferable?"

Lila sees Spence cringe. Nancy has always asked questions and done things differently, just to be contrary. "Nancy, Nancy, quite contrary," they used to tease her.

The doctor shrugs and leans against the wall. "It depends on a number of factors," he says. "You can't reduce it to a question of size. If it's an aggressive tumor, a fast-growing one, then a smaller lump might be more dangerous than one that has grown slowly over a longer period of time. And my suspicion is that this is an aggressive tumor. You can get a second opinion if you want to, but we've got her prepped, and if the second opinion was in favor of a lumpectomy, then wouldn't you have to go for a third opinion, so you could take two out of three? But in this case, time is of the essence." The doctor grins at Lila. "What do you think, Mrs. Culpepper? You look like a pretty smart lady."

"Why, you're just a little whippersnapper," Lila says. "All the big words make me bumfuzzled. I guess you know your stuff, but I got you beat when it comes to producing pretty daughters." She has heard he is single, and she heard the nurses joking with him. She can't keep her mind on the conversation. It's as though she's floating around the room, dipping in and out of the situation, the way the nurses do.

"That's for certain," he says, twirling his stethoscope like a toy.

"My daughters are curious, though," Lila says apologetically. Even the outfits they are wearing are curious—layers of dark, wrinkled cotton.

"They're weird," Spence says.

"No, we're not," says Cat indignantly. She's dressed up in one of her man-catching outfits, with heavy jewelry, but what man would like that getup? Cat claims women actually dress for women. Nancy was always too impatient to fool with her appearance. She's like Lila that way, wearing any old thing handy. When Nancy moved up north she stopped wearing lipstick and curling her hair, and for a while she didn't even wear a brassiere. Lila was afraid Nancy's breasts would be damaged.

"Do you have any questions, Mr. Culpepper?" the doctor asks. "Is there anything I can clarify?"

Lila senses Spence's embarrassment as he shakes his head no. The nurses are whizzing around, and the woman in the other bed is arguing with her doctor.

"What about them strokes?" Spence pipes up then.

"Well, the first priority is to deal with this lump in her breast, and later we'll check the obstructions in the carotid arteries." The doctor touches his neck, indicating the main blood vessels. He says, "It's possible that I'll recommend further surgery next week to clean out the plaque in those arteries."

"I was having strokes in Florida," Lila says. She

touches her arm, where the numbness spreads a few times a day. As they talk, she feels one of her dizzy spells coming on. She longs for a cigarette.

"How risky is that second operation?" Cat demands.

"Well, there's always the risk of death," the doctor says bluntly. He's not looking at anyone. His eyes are fixed on the doorframe. "And a carotid endarterectomy is tricky because there's always the chance the patient will have a stroke on the table. But the benefits outweigh the risks. Increase the blood supply to the brain and she'll stop having those transischemic attacks, and we'll prevent the big stroke down the road."

"The big stroke down the road," Nancy repeats, after he leaves. "It sounds like the title of a children's book."

Spence seems frozen in his position in the corner chair. His eyes stare vacantly as a nurse comes in with a syringe in her hand like a weapon. "Are you ready, Mrs. Culpepper?"

"Oh, must I?"

"It'll all be over with before you know it."

"Y'all messed up my fishing trip," Lila says crossly, trying to manage a smile. "I was aiming to go fishing this week."

"That's why we call you patients—because you have to be patient," the nurse says cheerfully. "Now you want to lie back for me? And make a fist."

From out of nowhere, Lila can hear Spence telling about the war, about a guy on his ship who went ashore one night on one of the Pacific islands and got himself tattooed. Spence wrote in his letter, "He had his whole butt tattooed with a picture of two beagles in a field—a pretty field, with green grass. And the dogs were after a rabbit that was disappearing into his crack. The next day the bos'n made him chip paint all day, and he hurt so bad he cried. It was a pretty picture, though, the grass was just as green! But I sure bet that hurt. He's a big guy too." She's about to laugh, remembering that letter.

She sees the girls whispering. The patient in the other bed is up walking again, but she refused her breakfast. Lila's breakfast was ice water. She wasn't hungry anyway. Food doesn't taste right to her anymore. The food on her trip to New Orleans back in March was unappetizing. The gumbo even had shells in it. Now Nancy is bending over her, hugging her, followed by Cat, her face close to Lila's. Cat whispers, "Hang in there, Mom." Spence is edging out the door as the orderlies appear with a bed on wheels. In their green outfits, they are leprechauns. Or men from Mars. "Are you going to give me some sugar or not?" Lila calls to Spence.

"I reckon," he says, clutching her hand and bending down to kiss her. He's self-conscious, but the nurse is busy filling out a chart and doesn't notice them.

"Take care of my babies," she says, meaning the cat and dog. "And don't forget them beans."

"I won't forget your old beans!" He chokes on his laugh.

As the leprechauns wheel her away, she sees Spence gazing after her helplessly. She has forgotten to tell Nancy and Cat something, something important she meant to say about Spence. His face disappears and she is in an elevator, with music playing, the kind of music they play in heaven.

$\mathcal{S}$PENCE can't stand hospitals. The smells
make him sick. The sounds of pain hurt. In an hour, the
doctor will telephone Lila's room with the biopsy report,
which will determine how he should proceed with the
surgery. Spence hates waiting.

He drives to a gas station that has a mini-market.
There, he buys two baked potatoes with cheese topping
and eats them in the car with a can of Coke. He plays the
radio, his rock station. The potatoes need more pepper.
Nancy and Cat urged him to eat in the cafeteria with
them, but he had little appetite in a building with so many
sick people and their germs. In the corridor when he arrived at the hospital that morning, Spence saw a man with
a hole in his face where his nose had been. Spence knows
a man who went to the cancer specialists in Memphis and
had a new nose grafted on. His face doesn't look bad with
the new nose, considering it came from a dead man. When
Spence told Nancy about it, she didn't believe him. Nancy
always believes what she wants to believe. He smiles,
thinking of how the doctor outsmarted her when she tried
to challenge him. Spence is proud of his daughter, though.
She has an important job—something to do with comput-
ers—with a company that requires her to travel all over
the United States. When Nancy married Jack Cleveland,
a Yankee, Spence was sure she was making a mistake. He
was afraid there wasn't a living in photography—more of

a hobby than work—but the marriage has lasted, and Robert is a smart, good-looking boy. It pains Spence that Nancy lives so far away. She went up there right after college. She was always restless and adventurous, because of the books she read. When she was little, she would read the same book over and over, as if she could make it come true.

Spence finishes the potatoes, gasses up the car, then drives to an auto-supply store to buy a windshield-wiper blade refill, but he can't find the right length and he doesn't want to buy a whole new wiper. He needs to get a tune-up, but he forgot to bring the coupon he clipped from the newspaper for a free one. He tries to calculate whether he would come out ahead if he went instead to that filling station offering the free case of Coke with a tune-up. But he doesn't have time to fool with the car today anyway. Impatiently, he drives back to the hospital, the radio blasting out rock-and-roll. The music fits the urgency of his life. The music seems to organize all the noises of public places into something he can tolerate. The rhythm of driving blends with the music on the radio and the beat in his nervous system. Before the children were born, he and Lila used to go dancing at little places out in the country that people called "nigger juke joints." They went to one across the county line where they could get beer. Lila never liked beer, but she loved to dance. He can imagine her long legs now, flashing white in the dark of the dance floor. He remembers a saxophone player and a blues singer as good as Joe Williams. The real music is always hidden somewhere, off in the country, back in his head, in his memory. There are occasional echoes of that raunchy old music he always loved in some of the rock songs on the radio.

At the hospital, he is forced to park in the last row.

"Midnight Rambler" by the Rolling Stones comes on the radio then, and he sits there and listens until it is finished. His family is busting out at the seams—like the music. He can't keep track of what they are up to. When a plane crash is on the news, he's afraid Nancy was on the plane. And Cat's life is a mess. She married too young, and her husband had big ideas he couldn't follow through on. He managed a hardware store, then opened his own water-bed outlet, but it failed. Spence told Cat the day Dan leased the store that waterbeds were filled with snake oil, not water, and she was mad at him for a long time for saying that. Lila tried to talk Cat into staying with Dan, but Spence is glad she got rid of him. Lila worries about Cat and the kids alone at night, with no man around the house, but Lila isn't afraid to go gallivanting around the world herself.

When Spence's mother died a few years ago, they were free to travel. By then, they had sold off the cows and weren't tied down on the farm. Spence told Lila he was going to send her around the world. She begged him to go too, but he refused to go traveling with a bunch of old people, yammering about their ailments. "I ain't that old," he protested.

"But we couldn't light out by ourselves," she said. "We'd get knocked in the head and robbed. We'd get lost. On these tours, they take care of you."

He was afraid for her to go off, but he wanted her to have the chance. Her first trip was to Hawaii, and at home alone he imagined her out on the Pacific, in a cruise boat that stopped at Pearl Harbor. When she came home from Hawaii, she brought a certificate for a hula-dancing course (three lessons) and some ceramic pineapples. "Did you get scared?" he asked. "Not a bit," she said. "I slept good, had the biggest time of my life." The airplane, she said, was

[47]

big enough to play ball in. On her second trip, a bus tour out to the Badlands, she brought him a toy rabbit with antlers—a jackelope. It was a joke present, but she wouldn't admit it, insisting she saw a jackelope cross the highway. After that, she went on two more trips, and when relatives commented snidely about how his wife was running around on him and spending all his money, it made him furious. He told them, "She took care of my mother for ten years, and she deserves to get out and have fun. If she wants to go to the moon, I'll let her. I don't care how much it costs."

While she was away in Hawaii, his memories of the Pacific grew louder, more insistent. The sounds of the antiaircraft guns echoed and reverberated below deck, where he was an ammunition passer. Storms battled the ship relentlessly, slopping the decks and plunging and hurtling the ship like a carnival ride. In the dark, cramped quarters—stinking with B.O. and puke—he tried to sleep, but he thought about Lila, nursing the baby and helping his parents get the crops in. He could see her milking the few cows they had during the war, washing the milk cans. One calm, sunny day, he carried buckets of water to swab the deck and forgot momentarily where he was, imagining he was carrying buckets of milk from the barn to the house. Then a fighter plane zoomed down low over the destroyer to land on the aircraft carrier a few hundred yards off the port bow.

When Spence enters Lila's room, the girls are reading magazines. The air-conditioning is cold. He's in a short-sleeved shirt, but they are wrapped up in layers of clothes.

"We stole her cigarettes," Cat says. "She had five packs at the bottom of her bag."

Nancy seems smaller each time he sees her, while Cat fattens up like a Butterball turkey. Cat has on a wrinkled jumpsuit with buttons and zippers all over it, and a wide belt with three buckles, and several pounds of beads. Nancy has on a sweater and a jacket and baggy pants with buttons at the ankles. This is July.

"Where did y'all get them clothes?" he says. "The rag barrel?"

Cat lets out a giggle. "One of the doctors called us 'honky Shiite terrorists.' "

Spence's daughters have never acted their age, but in a way he doesn't mind—they are still his little girls. He may burst into tears. Feeling a pang of heartburn, he sits down and grabs a section of the *Courier-Journal* from the floor. Too late, he thinks about the germs on the floor.

A nurse flies in and says to Nancy, "I'll have to ask you to get off the bed, hon. It's for the patient."

"I was warming it up for her," Nancy grumbles. She folds her reading glasses and slips them into a case.

"Y'all are always arguing with the doctors and nurses," Spence says to his daughters after the nurse leaves. "Talking back to them."

"Well, if we left it up to you, who knows what could happen to Mom!" Nancy says, sitting up on the edge of the bed and reaching for her shoes. "She could get mutilated. A lot of doctors just want to operate because they're enamored with their equipment." Nancy situates herself on a spread-out newspaper on the floor. "Let me ask you one thing, Dad. If you were in the hospital hooked up to tubes and you weren't even conscious, or maybe you were in excruciating pain—what would you want us to do?"

"I'm afraid of what y'all might have them doctors do to me." Spence shudders.

"Well, maybe you ought to think about it," Nancy says. "While you're still in charge."

"I'll solve that one," he says. "I just won't go to doctors. You're right about them anyway. They just want to work you over and take your money." He folds the newspaper and drops it to the floor. He says to Cat, "I believe your mama is more worried about you than she is about this operation."

"Well, I don't know what to do about it. She didn't see Scott laying on the ground that time. I thought he was dead!"

"He wasn't hurt."

"But Lee never should have let Scott ride that dumb three-wheeler. He was too little, and he didn't have a helmet. Those things are dangerous, the way kids ride them all over creation."

For a moment Spence sees Lila in his daughter. Lila swinging in a porch swing the night they married, her shoulder pads sticking out like scaffolding.

Cat goes on, "When I took Scott to the hospital, his fingers were numb—that's a sign of concussion. There was a kid killed just last week on a three-wheeler. Didn't you see that in the paper?"

Spence shakes his head in despair. It was an accident, and Lee was scared too. He says, "That's not what I meant. Lila's just worried about you—staying by yourself at night."

"What does she want me to do—bring some guy home with me?"

The telephone trills just then and Cat snatches it up. "Yes. Yes." She listens grimly.

"What is it?" Nancy says, motioning anxiously to Cat. "Is she O.K.?"

Cat nods. When she hangs up, she says, "The biopsy showed it was malignant, and he's going ahead with the mastectomy."

Spence's stomach lurches. "Oh, no," he says faintly.

His heart is racing. Nancy says nothing. Cat picks at her nails.

"They won't have her back up here till she gets out of the recovery room," Cat says. "It could be hours."

"Let's get out of here," Nancy says. "Let's go do something." She rolls her magazine and plunges it into her tote bag.

Cat, feeling for something in her purse, says, "I knew she had cancer when I saw her after she came back from Florida. I could see it in her face."

＊ ＊ ＊

Later, in the lounge, Spence spins through all the TV channels, but there are no ball games on today. The Cards are having a good season, especially with Joe Magrane, a Kentucky boy, pitching. Spence settles on a game show, but in his mind he sees her garden, with the corn growing full, and he sees her coming to the house early in the morning with buckets of vegetables. Her straw hat is set cockeyed on her head, and her blouse is damp. She bends over in the shade of the big oak and sorts through handfuls of shell beans, picking out some dried ones to save for seed. The cat twines himself around her ankles and she talks to him softly and sweetly, praising him for his morning's exploits. Behind her, the soybeans stretch out like a dusty green rug. The soybeans have been invaded by grasshoppers, and Spence is afraid of losing the crop. He never had a problem with grasshoppers before he switched to one-crop farming. His neighbor, Bill Belton, promised to spray the beans soon. Bill has a little crop-duster plane and won't charge Spence much. He has been kidding Spence about going up in the plane with him, but Lila won't hear of Spence going up. Spence has thought about it, though, imagining what it would be like to see

[51]

the fields from up high, with the pond like a glass eye and the buildings like dollhouses. He has never been up in an airplane.

He goes to the rest room and washes his teeth. Some of the potato is under the upper plate and starting to irritate the roof of his mouth. Earlier, he was in such a hurry to get back to Lila's room he didn't wash his teeth. On the commode, he smokes half a cigarette. For the last several years, he has limited himself to two cigarettes a day. But he can't stop Lila. She puffs away like the smoke-stack in the industrial park beyond the soybean fields. Sometimes he watches her puffing and sees the smoke-stack puffing simultaneously, and they are like coordinated events in his life, events he has no control over. He runs water at the sink over the cigarette butt and drops it in the waste can.

In the hall, he runs into Guy Samson, a man he sees often at the feed mill. Spence used to rent Guy's bulls.

"Spence, have you got somebody here?" Guy asks.

"My wife," Spence says, feeling himself tremble. "She's being operated on. Breast cancer."

"That's tough, Spence," Guy says, shaking his head worriedly. "My mother-in-law's here now with cancer, and she's real bad. She's hooked up to them machines in intensive care."

"They're hooking everybody up these days."

"Ain't that the truth. Does your wife have to have cobalt?"

Spence shudders. "They haven't said." He knows that with cancer they will give her cobalt treatments, and he has tried to put this out of his mind.

"That cobalt is what I'd be afraid of," Guy says, nodding his head sympathetically.

Spence is shivering in the cold.

"Take it easy, Spence," says Guy as they part.

The word "cobalt" stung Spence to the quick. He has known people who had cobalt. Claudine Turrell lost her hair and was sick from radiation poisoning, like the Japanese after the bomb. Claudine finally died, after suffering for weeks. The same thing happened to Bob Miller and Clancy Stone. And Lila's friend Reba died only last year, after several rounds of cobalt treatments. It occurs to Spence now that Lila has not even mentioned Reba, as if it would be bad luck to say her name. Lila visited Reba in the hospital and came home describing Reba's bald head and skinny neck—a picked chicken, Lila said sadly.

The doctors would say, "These cobalt treatments might give her a little time." There is no choice about it, really. There are no significant choices most of the time. You always have to do what has to be done. It's like milking cows. When their bags are full, they have to be milked.

SIX

*L*ILA FEELS a twitching on the back of her hand, like a fly that has landed, but she is unable to swat at it. Then she feels the tube hanging out of her hand. She eases open her eyes, sees blurred faces and machines with hoses—like the electric milkers they used to have for the cows. Her eyes close and she sees green beans setting on blooms again and okra poking up like hitchhikers' thumbs. A volunteer sunflower has sprung up amidst the peppers. There is a burning in her chest, a smoldering fire in a woodstove. Something bulky is there, a heavy weight holding her down. She is too weak to bring her hand up to touch it. A TV set, somewhere near, seems to be playing a story about a woman's best friend dying of cancer. The friend's name is Reba, and they play cards and go fishing together. Reba is smart and has a giggle like a little girl. One day Reba finds a lump the size of a golf ball in her breast. She claims it came there overnight, but she is lying. Reba kept it a secret, hadn't wanted to admit it was there. She had such tiny breasts, not like Lila's large, knotty breasts. A golf ball could hide in Lila's unnoticed. Reba's hair falls out and she wastes away to nothing and disappears beyond the garden.

Someone wheels a cart into the room. Lila hears tinkling glass, the sucking of rubber soles, voices bubbling. The sound of the TV story has faded away. Outlines of people grow sharper, faces peering quizzically at her. Lila does not want them staring at her. She must look awful.

$\mathcal{A}$LL THE WAY to the hospital the next day, Spence listens to tapes of the Blasters and Fleetwood Mac that Nancy brought for him. The Fleetwood Mac tape doesn't even sound like Fleetwood Mac. He wouldn't have recognized the group. The Blasters remind him of Jerry Lee Lewis. Spence saw Jerry Lee Lewis on a special recently. He looked bad—old and worn out.

He dreads seeing Lila, so he has fooled around half the morning, delaying the trip to Paducah. In Paducah, before going to the hospital, he looks for a gallon of windshield-washer fluid and has to go to a couple of places to compare prices. He pays four dollars for it. Later, in the Wal-Mart, where he stops to look for that wiper-blade replacement, he spots the same brand of washer fluid on sale for two dollars. He has blown two bucks. It makes him mad. All the coffee makers and video games and electric ice-cream parlors in the Wal-Mart are depressing. People are buying so much junk, thinking it will make them happy. And then when they can't even make a path across the floor through their possessions, they have a yard sale. Spence can't stand to waste anything. His parents never wasted a scrap. "Always be saving," Pap told his grandchildren. "Hard times might come." Cat fought him, pitching a fit once over two shelly beans left on her plate. These days, with all the new money, everyone has gone wild. Around here, there is nowhere to go, so people either get drunk or go crazy—sometimes both. Spence knows a guy whose wife left him and ran off to Biloxi, Mississippi, with a prefab-home builder whom she later shot dead. After that, the guy had a nervous breakdown and was sent off to the asylum. The children went to foster homes. Spence can't imagine what the world is coming to. Yesterday, the newspaper reported two burglaries in town—a holdup at an all-night food store and a break-in at an old widow's house.

In the Wal-Mart parking lot, he has a sudden queasy feeling. He can't remember where he is. He sees rows and rows of cars. His brain reels. He must have a car here, but he can't remember what car. He sees a Camaro, an Oldsmobile, rows of shiny silver and white cars, lined up like teeth. The vertical lines of street lamps tower in the landscape like defoliated trees. The parking lot seems slightly familiar, but he can't place it. He may be thinking of one he has seen on TV. He stumbles onward and suddenly spots his car—the Rabbit that needs a tune-up. The little car seems to have aged ten years overnight. It is parked next to a black van with round windows and a pink-and-blue mural of an angel and a Jesus with a halo. Spence wonders what loony drives such a vehicle. Spence has never been comfortable in church. He is suspicious of most preachers and believes all the evangelists on the radio and TV are con artists. The night before, when Lila came out of the recovery room and was wheeled back into Room 301, she said to him, "Did you pray for me?" Her question startled him. They never spoke of prayer, or heaven, but Spence knew she prayed for him, frequently, because she went to church and was afraid that because he didn't they wouldn't end up in heaven together. When he answered her, he felt a chill up his spine. "Sure," he

said, joking. "You know how good I am at saying grace."
She got tickled at him then but had to stop laughing
because she hurt. "I've got a long row to hoe," she said.
She wasn't fully awake.

$\mathcal{L}$ILA FEELS as though she has been left out in a field for the buzzards. The nurses are in at all hours, making no special effort to be quiet—a nurse who checks dressings, another one who changes dressings, a nurse with blood-thinner shots three times a day, a nurse with breathing-machine treatments, various nurses' aides who check temperature and blood pressure, the cleaning woman, the mail lady, the priest and nuns from the hospital, the girls who fill the water jugs, the woman who brings the meal trays, the candy stripers selling toiletries and candy and magazines from a cart. Lila can't keep track of all the nurses who come to check her drainage tube— squirting the murky fluid out of the plastic collection bottle, measuring the fluid intake and output, writing on charts. The nurses walk her around the entire third floor twice a day, accompanied by her I.V. bag, wheeling on a stand. Spence is nervous, bursting in anxiously, unable to stick around. And the girls are in and out, bringing her little things—a basket of flowers from the gift shop downstairs and some perfume. Lee and Joy brought a rose in a milk-glass bud vase. The church sent pink daisies. The old woman in the other bed has no flowers.

The surgeon told Lila she could live without a breast. "You couldn't live without a head, or a liver, or a heart," he said when he informed her in the recovery room that he had removed her breast. "But you can live without a breast. You'll be surprised."

"It would be like living without balls," Lila replied. "You'd find that surprising too, but you could probably get along without them."

Lila is not sure she said that aloud, and remembering it now, she is embarrassed that she might have, under the influence of the drugs. She's surprised Nancy hasn't said the same thing to the doctor's face.

Lila hears the old woman in the other bed grunting and complaining. "I'll not leave here alive!" she shouted when a nurse gave her a bath. "You're wasting your time fooling with me."

By the second day after her surgery, Lila is no longer hooked to the I.V. She plucks at the hospital gown in front where her bandage itches. The drainage tubes irritate her skin. She feels weak, but restless. "I'm afraid my blood's too thin already," she tells the nurse who comes with the blood-thinner shot.

"No, this is what the doctor wanted," the nurse says.

"I'm getting poked so full of holes I'm like a sifter bottom."

Besides the shots, there are the tests. They have wheeled her into the cold basement three times to run her through their machines. They have scanned her bones, her liver, her whole body, looking for loose cancer cells. Now the cancer doctor comes in to tell Lila the results of the tests: The cancer has spread to two out of the seventeen lymph nodes that were removed. Spence isn't there yet, but Cat and Nancy fire questions at him. Lila's head spins as the doctor explains that once the cancer has reached the lymph nodes, it has gone into the bloodstream, and then it can end up anywhere. The news doesn't quite register.

"I'm recommending chemotherapy," the doctor says.

"Is that cobalt?" Lila asks weakly. The doctor is young and reminds her of the odd-looking preacher who led the revival at church last year. The preacher had a long nose and wore a gold shiny suit.

The doctor says, "No. This will be a combination of three drugs—Cytoxan, methotrexate and 5FU." He explains that she will have a chart showing two weeks of treatments, then a three-week rest period, then two weeks of treatments, and so on. She will get both pills and shots. Like dogs teaming up on a rabbit, Cat and Nancy jump on him about side effects.

"This particular treatment is tolerated very well," he says. "That's not to say there won't be side effects. A little hair loss, a little nausea. Some people react more adversely than others."

Lila can't keep her mind on what he's saying. "I've got plenty of hair," she says, tugging at her curls. "And it's coarse, like horse hair." The last permanent she got didn't take on top.

"You're going to have to lay off the smoking too," the doctor says, consulting his clipboard.

"They won't let me smoke here," Lila says. She bummed a cigarette from a visitor in the lounge the night before, but it burned her lungs and tasted bitter. She couldn't finish it.

The cancer doctor says now, "Cigarettes will interfere with the chemotherapy."

"See!" Nancy says triumphantly. "Doctor's orders. And you wouldn't listen to us."

"These girls snitched my cigarettes," Lila says to the doctor. "Is that any way to treat an old woman that's stove up in the hospital?"

"Best thing for you," the doctor says with a slight grin.

"And they're telling me I can't eat what I'm used to," Lila goes on.

"She eats a high-fat diet," Nancy says.

"Don't listen to them," the doctor says to Lila. "You eat anything you want to. If I was your age, I'd eat anything I wanted to."

Lila sees Nancy bristle. Nancy says, "She's eaten bacon and eggs every morning of her life and she has clogged arteries. What are you saying?"

"It's too late for her to do anything about her diet. Cutting back on cholesterol won't help at all. It's simply too late. And it's too late for you too," he says. "How old are you?"

"Forty-four."

"Too late." He nods at Cat. "How old are you?"

"Thirty-four."

"It might help you a little, but not much. They did autopsies on the soldiers who died in Vietnam, and those young boys—nineteen years old—already had plaque in their arteries."

"Not all doctors agree with you about cholesterol," Nancy says, shooting him a mean look.

As he scribbles on his chart, the doctor tells a complicated story about some experiments on Italian women conducted with the drugs he is prescribing. Nancy and Cat follow him out into the hall. Lila suspects they are keeping something from her. She doesn't know what to think. The doctor didn't say if she would be cured, and she was afraid to ask.

She can feel the wound draining, little drips that tickle. The nurses don't use any kind of ointment on it. When she was a child, she had an infected place where she had stuck a stob in her shin. Her aunt Dove bought some

Rosebud salve from a peddler and it healed the sore. Lila remembers when they used to rub dirt in wounds; dirt was pure, what grew things. Good dirt was precious.

In the other bed, the old woman yells at the nurse bringing her lunch tray.

"You can just take that right back, because I don't want it."

"If you don't start eating for us, we'll have to put you back on the I.V., Mrs. Wright," the nurse says in a tone one would use to a child.

The nurse disappears into the hall and comes back with Lila's dinner.

"Oh, no, not more food," Lila says.

Spence, looking tired and cold, comes in a little later. She is still picking at her dinner.

"The doctor said it spread to two out of seventeen lymp' nodes," Lila tells him. Before she can respond to Spence's shocked expression, Cat and Nancy return and tell him what the doctor said.

"He's going to try chemotherapy," Cat says.

"Cobalt?"

"No."

Spence grins, the worry on his face lifting. "I was afraid they were going to do cobalt. I couldn't sleep none all night, thinking about it."

"No. Just shots and pills."

Spence says, "What'll it do?"

"He wouldn't say."

"He was optimistic," Nancy assures Spence.

Cat repeats what the doctor said about the treatment. Lila, amazed that anyone can remember all that, notices that Cat doesn't go into detail about the discussion on fat. Spence listens without comment.

Lila shoves her tray at Spence. "Here, does anybody want some of this turkey? I can't go another bite."

"That mess looks awful." He turns up his nose.

"We're going to the cafeteria," Nancy says. "Why don't you come with us, Daddy?"

He shakes his head. "I found this place with baked taters four for a dollar."

"*Four* baked potatoes?" Cat asks.

"I just get two," he says. "And a Coke and some peanuts."

"You better go down to the cafeteria," Lila says to him, "and get you some meat and vegetables. I can't say much for their cooking, though."

"You can say that again," Mrs. Wright in the other bed says, her voice calling through the curtain partition. "They call this turkey and dressing? It ain't even Thanksgiving. We had better grub at the poorhouse when I used to work in the kitchen."

Lila says, "You better eat it, though, to keep body and soul together."

"I told 'em I wasn't eating a bite and I won't. I'll not leave this hospital alive anyway."

Spence and Cat and Nancy grin at each other. Cat whispers to Spence, "She's been going on like that all morning."

A nurse says, "I'll be back to check your drainage when you're done eating."

"They never leave you alone," says Lila. "All night long they come in. 'Mrs. Culpepper? Time to take your temperature.' 'Mrs. Culpepper? Time to check the drainage.' They come in here and wake me up just to refill the water jug."

"They go by their rules," Nancy says. "They don't care about you as a person."

"There's one nurse that's cute as a bug's ear," Lila says. "She tickles me. She's got a cute disposition and the littlest feet."

"Isn't Mom doing great?" Cat says to Spence with a grin.

"She's got her fire back," Spence says, beaming at Lila.

"This place ain't seen nothing yet," says Lila. "I'm tough as nails and rough as a cob!" She laughs at herself and feels the bandage pull her skin. She wants to be cheerful, for the girls, but she doesn't feel cheerful.

In the afternoon, when the girls have gone, a nurse draws back the curtain partition, and the sunlight through the window next to Mrs. Wright's bed floods Lila's side of the room. The TV is playing a soap opera about a woman whose husband is having an affair with their adopted daughter.

"I hate them old stories," Mrs. Wright says. "The same thing ever' day, and it never does come to an end."

"They just want to keep you going on them," Lila says. The adopted daughter on TV is pregnant now. She has agreed to be a surrogate mother for her adoptive parents, who can't have children.

"My belly steeples is itching," says Mrs. Wright. "I feel like yanking 'em out."

"Don't you have any family close by to come and see you?" Lila asks. The woman has had no visitors.

"None except my brother, but he's in Tennessee. And he don't care a rat's behind what happens to me. There's a bunch of nieces and nephews and their littluns—just little tadpoles."

Lila says, "I've raised three fine younguns." She fumbles for the remote-control box by the bed and turns down the sound of the soap opera.

Mrs. Wright says, "I've farmed all my life except for

a year when I went to Detroit and worked during the war. I've gone out in the morning when the dew was dried off and cut hay and baled it and got it in before it rained. We'd work till ten or eleven at night."

"I always helped hay too," Lila says. "You ain't got nothing on me."

"I lifted the bales right into the truck just like a man. Did you lift bales into the truck?"

"Well, I *drove* the truck," says Lila. "They wouldn't let me lift like that—in case my insides might drop."

"That could be the cause of my trouble," Mrs. Wright says. "I wouldn't have come to this place, but they bellyached and bellyached till they got me here. I could have got along fine without them cutting me open."

"Who bellyached?"

"Oh, them people I rent my trailer from."

The woman rattles on, but Lila pretends to be falling asleep. In the TV story, the adopted daughter is driving over a bridge. The bridge railing breaks. Debris scatters, gray water rolling with bits of wreckage. Then an instant soup is steaming in a cup and a bleached-blond woman in a shiny kitchen is smiling. Lila's kitchen is not that fancy, even though they remodeled a few years ago, but she remembers how proud she was to get out of Rosie's miserable, dark kitchen, with the dishwater simmering on the gas stove. By the time Cat was born, Lila and Spence had built their own house, a hundred yards away from his parents' house, through the woods. They had two dozen cows by then, and the dairy prospered. Rosie churned butter; Lila helped with the milking and bottling; Spence made the deliveries in town; Amp and Spence raised corn and hay. In her new house, a plain four-room square, Lila had her own kitchen, with running water. With her blackberry money, she bought a pressure cooker. Later, they bought a freezer and installed indoor plumbing, and eventually they added more rooms. Lila relaxed and let things go. She didn't yell at the kids for strewing their clothes and toys everywhere. She spoiled them. Before Easter Sunday, she often found herself staying up past midnight finishing their Easter outfits. And she made so many clothes for Cat over the years she could have stocked a store. Her children were always well fed and wore good clothes.

The house she grew up in had a sort of unfinished feeling to it. Some of the rooms upstairs were bare wood walls, with the studs showing, and the family itself felt unfinished. It shot off in different directions—in-laws, cousins, widows, a cousin with an illegitimate child, an aunt whose husband had abandoned her. Uncle Mose took in strays like Lila, anybody with a pair of hands to help him work his tobacco, but Lila always felt she was just an extra mouth to feed. When she married Spence and moved in with his parents, she felt out of place. Their house was dark and filled with silences. Rosie even shelled beans with great concentration, as if chatter would be inefficient. Lila tried to fit in, as she had learned to do in a large household of grownups, but when Amp and Rosie stepped on her feelings, or made her feel unworthy because she didn't know how to do things their way, there were no aunts or cousins to run to. At Uncle Mose's, in that big clumsy bunch, she was the youngest, and she had to play by herself. She tied doll bonnets on cats and packed them, squirming, from place to place. A cat drowned in the cistern once. The men drained the cistern, and her cousin Dulcie, who bossed everybody, made Lila descend a ladder into that dark pit to get the dead cat. "You're so crazy about cats, you're the right one to send," Dulcie said in a practical tone. Lila brought the cat up in her arms, slimy and already rotting, and for a long time after that the water wasn't fit to drink, but they washed in it. Even now, whenever Lila sees a dead cat she recalls that cat in the cistern.

As Lila is waking up, later in the afternoon, Nancy appears with a cup of coffee, and the old woman says to her, "You'll be high, wide and handsome about eleven o'clock tonight if you drink that."

"How are you doing, Mrs. Wright?" Nancy asks.

"I'm still swelled, but he looked at it and said I was doing good. But I'm not."

"Did you eat your lunch?"

"No. That hospital food ain't fitten to eat—no seasoning."

"You didn't touch a bite," Lila reminds her sleepily. "So how do you know it wasn't any good?"

"I could tell by looking." Mrs. Wright heaves her heavy blue-and-white legs over the edge of the bed and faces the window. "Nobody'll ever talk me into going in the hospital again."

Nancy sets her coffee on the night table and clasps Lila's hand. Lila feels strength flowing into her arm from her daughter, and she holds Nancy's hand tightly.

"Do you want me to read to you?" Nancy asks. "Cat had to go to work. She said she'd be back at six."

"No, that's all right. I couldn't keep my mind on it."

"How do you feel?"

"There's too much commotion going on here to think," Lila says. She pulls at the front of her gown.

Nancy touches the limp curls that droop onto her mother's forehead. "I think it looks very promising," Nancy says. "They caught it early and they can do wonders nowadays."

[71]

A nurse, appearing suddenly, closes the curtain partition between the two beds. "Mrs. Culpepper? We need to check your dressing."

The nurse shoos Nancy out and pulls another curtain around the bed. She pokes at the bandage and peels it back. Lila doesn't want to look, but she glimpses a brown spot. She wonders if they saved her nipple. Cat mentioned earlier that if they saved her nipple they could rebuild her breast. The brown spot is far off center.

NINE

HE WAY doctors throw their forty-dollar
words around like weapons is infuriating. Spence knows
big words, plenty of them. He prefers not to use his vo-
cabulary in conversation, though, for fear of sounding
pretentious. Using the right simple words at the right time
requires courage enough. At times there is no way on
earth he can say what he feels.

He knows what he *wants* to say, and he imagines saying it to Lila, but it takes guts to admit guilt and wrong,
to express sorrow, to lavish loving feelings on someone.
If only he could, he would say, "Lila, you and me have
been together a long time, and we've been through a lot
together." He laughs to himself. How phony that would
be. It sounds like something on television. He has never
said those things because he would feel as though he were
speaking lines. Real love requires something else, something deeper. And sometimes a feeling just goes without
saying.

Show her you love her, they say. Doesn't he show her?
Everything he does is for her, even when he goes his own
way and she is powerless to stop him—like the time he
drove the tractor across the creek after it had washed out
and she was afraid the tractor would turn over. As he
headed out through the field to the creek, she called and
called, but he wouldn't stop. He has always teased her
about her habit of worrying herself sick over nothing.

Teasing rattles her, but it would be out of character for him to behave any other way, and she would respect him less.

He could say to Lila, "It's all right. Your breast isn't your life. You can live without it, and I'll accept that." More lines. He has to show her another way, letting her know indirectly how much he still loves her. "Our love will never die." Words are so inadequate. Phony. Nobody he knows says things like that anyway. People either lie to be nice or they say what they think. The girls used to accuse Spence of being cruel when he spoke his mind, but that is not true. He is just honest. He hates hypocrites.

The morning after her operation, when he came in so late, afraid to see her, she was sitting up in bed, gabbing with a nurse as if nothing had happened. "Where in the world have you been?" she said to him accusingly. "I thought you'd forgot about me." She had on lipstick, and her hair was pretty, the color of straw. Later, he helped her walk down the corridor, pulling her I.V. along like a child's wagon, and she joked with him about her lost breast. She said, "I didn't realize how you depend on your jugs for balance. I feel all whopper-jawed! And I have to go around holding the other one up till I can wear a brassiere." Spence told her he could rig her up a sling, like the one he fashioned for a hound dog once when she had an open wound on the bottom of her paw.

When they made a turn at the end of the hallway, Lila suddenly asked him, "Why do you think this happened to me?"

"No reason. Things just happen. What do you mean?"

"I don't know. It just don't seem right."

Spence wanders through the house now, seeing her things. The collection of dolls she laboriously sewed clothes for, the knickknacks she bought at yard sales, her closet stuffed with pants suits and flowered dresses she made for herself, the rack of quilts she spent so many winters constructing. A casserole she made for him is still in the refrigerator, as well as a ham and bowls of green beans and stock peas. Neighbors brought Spence an odd assortment of dishes—coconut pie, lima beans cooked with macaroni, stewed tomatoes, green Jell-O streaked with shredded cabbage. Spence doesn't eat much in the evenings because food at night gives him heartburn, and he is at the hospital during the day, so the food is spoiling. It is depressing. If it were Lila's funeral, the same people would bring the same food.

He is walking to the pond with Oscar, escaping the chaos in the house. Nancy and Cat have come to clean, and they're rearranging everything. They moved his outdoor clothes out of the living room—his boots, his jackets, the manure-stained pants he wore for feeding the animals. Lila always let him keep the clothes by the door, where they were handy, but Nancy and Cat dumped them all— including his boots and bootjack—in a corner of the bedroom. "Honestly, Daddy," said Cat in exasperation. She handed him a slop bucket to take to the ducks.

"What do you think, Oscar?" he says aloud. At that moment, Oscar sees the ducks and bounds forward merrily. Oscar is a small gray dog with shaggy hair down in his eyes. "Get back here. Don't chase them ducks!" Spence shouts. On the pond bank, the ducks skitter ahead of Oscar and splash into the water. Oscar tests the water, then gets distracted by a grasshopper. Spence empties the slop bucket on the bank—rotting lettuce and blackening radishes and rubbery break beans from the vegetable crisper that Cat cleaned out. The ducks paddle to the bank and dart their bills furtively at the garbage. Oscar has gone down into the creek. Spence scans the pond bank for the hoofprints of deer. Recently he saw three deer crossing the field to the pond—a doe and two young ones. Spence has never shot a deer and does not plan to.

From a rise near the pond Spence surveys the ocean of soybeans, with the dips and waves in the front fields and the stripe of corn edging the back ten. The farm has seventy-three acres. He remembers his father teaching him how to figure while they worked the fields. Pappy drilled him in the multiplication table as they cultivated the rows of corn with a mule. When Spence was eight, he realized that when he was thirty-three Pappy would be sixty-six, twice his age. Now Spence is almost sixty-six himself. His father has been dead for fifteen years. Spence is glad Pappy did not live to see the milk cows sold off.

A grasshopper shoots through the air. The soybeans are thick with them. With no-till beans, he had to use a weed-killer a week after planting, and he suspects that it killed a certain weed the grasshoppers liked, so they are eating the new bean leaves instead. Bill Belton will have to spray soon. Besides the cropduster plane, Bill is deeply in debt for a combine and a planter. Spence has never gone into debt, but he knows a couple of farmers who have lost their land after overborrowing. When he took a part-time job, driving a van during the school year for the high school, he was able to get medical benefits, which will help now with Lila's illness. But he worries about whether it is enough. He might have to cash in his certificate of deposit, which doesn't mature until October. In his worst moments, he can imagine losing his farm to doctors.

On the edge of the field, he steps across a ridge of dirt pushed up by a tractor tire. A few stray soybeans perch on the top, and the tire print beside it is dry like a scar. He thinks of the furrow the doctors may cut in Lila's neck.

When he was looking at her things, he ran across a postcard she had written him from Savannah. It showed a picture of a lighthouse. When he got home from the Navy, she seemed stronger, tougher, and he felt weaker, torn apart. After the Navy, Spence never wanted to travel again. Home was like that lighthouse. At night on the ocean, the exploding artillery shells kept him awake. The seasickness was worse below deck. Swinging in his hammock, slamming against metal walls and poles, he wanted to die. The sounds down there were magnified—whistles, loudspeakers, the big thumps bombs made hitting water, feet running on deck, metal doors clanging shut. It was deafening. He never saw any of the battles. He knew when there was a battle because the lights turned red. He threw up on a five-inch shell on its way up to the gun turret. He never knew if the shells he touched found their way to the heart of an enemy craft. Up on deck, it was calmer: the fighter planes coming and going from the flat-top; the big ship protected in the huddle like a queen bee. It felt better out on deck, because he could see what was going on. He was where the weather was. The fighters landing on the carrier reminded him of snake doctors floating through the air, alighting on a weed, flitting off. A snake doctor touched down on his bare arm once when he was a child and left a blister as large as a nickel. In his nightmares out on the sea, the kamikazes made blisters on the deck of the destroyer and the ship exploded with fire. After he came home, he still couldn't sleep. He stayed up late and read about the battles, wanting to find out about the big battle he was in, but he couldn't find many books about the Pacific. Most of them were about Germany. He could see the battle in his mind's eye, from what he heard afterward, but there wasn't enough information in the books. He wanted to know how his destroyer fit in the larger picture, a whole world at war. He had so many questions about the Japanese, the islands, the atom bomb. He wanted to know every detail of what happened, how it happened, why. But the more he read, the more confusing it became, the larger it grew. He couldn't keep up the reading at night because he always had to get up so early to milk, and after that he faced a long day in the fields. Eventually, his eyes went bad and reading gave him terrible headaches. "Forget about that war," Lila told him. "It's over."

Last night he had a nightmare about Godzilla invading his soybeans. Now he imagines his fields barren and swampy, like the Everglades. He has heard that when the big earthquake expected in the Mississippi River Valley hits, everything for miles will turn to liquid clay.

❧   ❧   ❧

By the time Spence returns to the house, the girls have finished cleaning, and now they are freezing corn. Nancy is cutting corn off the cob, and Cat stirs corn in a skillet on the stove. Cookie pans spread with cooked corn are cooling in front of the air conditioner. The kitchen is steamy. Freezer bags litter the table.

"Ain't it too late in the day to pick corn?" he asks.

"We couldn't wait till tomorrow. It's getting too old," Cat says.

Nancy cuts the corn off the cob the way her mother taught her to do it years ago—first halfway through the kernels, then all the way, then scraping the cob for the juice. It has been years since Nancy has done this, and there is a frown on her face.

"Mom took the news about the chemotherapy real well," says Cat.

"She's more scared than she admits," Nancy says.

"She's really brave," Cat says. "But she's being extra brave for us."

"I'd go to pieces," Nancy says, viciously scraping the cob with the knife.

"I hope she stays off the cigarettes," Cat says.

"The cigarette tax is going up," Nancy says. "Reagan will just send the money to the contras."

Trying to stay busy, Spence collects the trash from the basement and starts burning it in the trash barrel behind the old milkhouse. The cloud of black smoke blows south, toward the smokestack of the industrial park. Spence likes that—he's sending the park a message, like Indians with smoke signals. Suddenly Nancy, the corn knife still in her hand, is standing there yelling at him.

"You're not supposed to burn those plastic Coke bottles!"

"But how am I going to get rid of them?"

"You'll have to dump them. You shouldn't buy that kind."

He throws some boxes on the fire, and angry, dark smoke boils up.

"Plastic releases polyvinyl chloride," she says. "It's a deadly pollutant."

"I don't want to dump too much trash in the creek."

Nancy runs inside the house, holding her nose, and he tosses the remaining plastic bottles onto the fire. The two-liter size is ninety-nine cents, a savings of a dollar-eleven over Coke in cans. He feels helpless. Nancy is so much like Lila. He remembers Lila chasing him with a mop all the way to the railroad track once. They were very young, and she was mad at him for tracking his muddy boots on the floor she had just mopped. He can still see her short, loose dress, her breasts swinging like fruit on a branch in a strong breeze.

TEN

L ILA FEELS the arteries in her neck throbbing, heavy with blood trying to reach her brain. Nancy claimed the blood vessels were stopped up with bacon grease. The bacon that comes with the hospital breakfast is usually burned, and Lila still has no appetite, but she tries to eat because it is wrong to waste food. She hasn't smoked. The thought of cigarettes makes her gag.

She doesn't believe the cancer has spread. She can't feel it anywhere. The doctor said the knot was only the size of a lima bean. She is self-conscious about the emptiness on her right front. The bandage itches, and the drainage tube irritates her. The tube coils out of the wound and connects to the plastic drainage bottle taped to her stomach, close to her shaved groin. She does not know why they had to shave her there. With the bottle flapping as she walks down the hall, she imagines that this is what a man's balls must be like. She pulls at the hospital gown, filling it out with air so she won't appear so lopsided. With the drainage bottle and her flattened chest, she might have had a sex-change operation. Her mind still seems cloudy at times, and then sometimes all the recent events come at her in a rush. She probably shouldn't have gone to Florida. She recalls Cat saying, "Lee and Daddy never should have taken you to the Everglades when it was off-season—ninety-eight degrees and wall-to-wall mosquitoes." Lila told Cat, "That cloud of mosquitoes was purely black!"

Losing her breast feels something like giving birth. Part of her that used to bulge out is now vacant, the familiar growth gone. It's an empty sensation, but not exceptionally painful. Now that she has been thinking about it, it seems natural, after all, that disease should attack her there, that she should be most vulnerable there. Probably she strained her breasts; they were too large; and she has had so much mastitis. It makes sense. When Lee was born, she was tired and overworked. During the winter she had been working at the clothing factory, and that summer she made several premature trips to the hospital, returning home empty-handed. It was frustrating, and when Lee was finally born, the other children stood beside her hospital bed accusingly, as if she had done something peculiar for her age. She was only thirty-two, but seeing Nancy, who was already twelve, made her feel old. Nancy pleaded, "Come home soon, because nobody will do what I say and I hate to cook." They didn't tell Lila until later about the scare with Cathy—as she was called then. She wasn't called Cat until that movie *Cat Ballou.* Cathy had disappeared, and they didn't find her for over two hours. She was walking down the railroad tracks, her face stained purple—probably from eating poisonous pokeberries. She was sick all night.

After Lila came home from the hospital with the baby, he cried so much at night that Spence started sleeping on his parents' screened-in porch. Lila realized Lee was hungry for solid food. She began feeding him baby food, as well as cow's milk in a bottle. For the only time in her life, Lila could barely manage. Vegetables from the garden were coming in, the blackberries were ripe, and Cat was still so little she had to be watched every minute. Nancy

[82]

was becoming difficult—moody and resentful of her chores. She played loud music on the radio. Lila got no sleep those first few months. But a few years later, they bought their first television, and an unexpected harmony filled the house. They gathered in the living room with a dishpan full of popcorn. Their favorite show was *I Love Lucy.* When Lucy broke into one of her childish bawls, Lee would pucker up and pretend to bawl too. "A great sense of humor for a kid," Nancy said. Lila recalled long winter nights at Uncle Mose's, when there was no entertainment to work by. There was only the bickering of her older cousins over the ironing and sewing, with Uncle Mose in his rocking chair, reading the Bible and farting, seemingly at will. Behind his back, they called him Old Whistle-britches.

Nancy is waving a large envelope in Lila's face. "Mom, I have something wonderful to show you. Jack just sent some new pictures of Robert."

"He's going to be a ladykiller," Cat says. "Nancy, I wish you'd brought him with you!"

"Oh, let me get my glasses," says Lila eagerly. She doesn't see her oldest grandchild often, but in the pictures Nancy frequently sends, Lila has watched him grow, like that kitten in the television commercial who changes into a grown cat in just a few seconds.

Nancy, removing the pictures from the envelope, says, "Jack sent them Federal Express to me at Cat's. He sent them last night and they got here this morning."

"I can't get over that," says Cat. "Anymore, everything's so fast."

Lila adjusts her glasses and examines the pictures as Nancy hands them to her one by one. They are large black-and-white pictures on thick paper, unlike the little snapshots the drugstore develops.

"He's filled out a lot," Lila says. "He don't look like a starved chicken anymore."

Robert seems confident and grown. In one picture, he's holding something, maybe keys, and in his sunglasses he's in a playful pose, pretending he's somebody famous. He's in dark pants and a T-shirt with faint writing on it.

"Isn't he darling?" Cat says. "I could just eat him up."

"He's about five-ten now," says Nancy. "Look at this one."

"That's my favorite," Cat says. "He looks like Daddy."

"Why, he does!" Lila studies the picture closely. She can see Spence hiding there—the firm lines of the jaw, the clenched teeth, the concealed beginning of a grin. Spence wasn't much older than Robert is now when she first saw him. He was riding a mule down Wolf Creek Road. His mother had cut his hair, causing his cowlick to shoot up like a tuft of grass on top of a stump, but it only accentuated his good looks. Lila gets tickled and laughs at Robert's hair. "I sure didn't know he had a cowlick," she says.

"It's not a cowlick. It's spiked," Nancy explains. "It's what kids do to their hair these days."

"Robert has your eyes," Lila says, noticing the dark glint in Nancy's eyes. "I always said he had your eyes."

Lila remembers the time Lee cut his foot on the jagged edge of a rusted coffee can that had been opened by one of those old-timey can openers. Lila knew from Nancy's scared eyes as she ran toward the house with Lee in her arms that something terrible had happened, even before she saw the blood from Lee's foot.

"And now for the prize." Nancy is hiding the last picture against her chest. "This is Robert at the end of the school year. They didn't have a prom. They had what they

call a 'superlative.' It's an honors thing, where they cele-
brate their achievements."

"I can't believe this," says Cat as Nancy turns the
picture face forward.

Robert, in a tuxedo, is standing against a doorway next
to a pretty girl in a long dress with a ruffle around the
neck. Both of them have that wild hair, standing up as if
electrified.

"He's girlfriending already!" Lila cries. "Law, that
hair."

"Her name is Amy," says Nancy. "Her mother is our
accountant."

"I bet all the girls are crazy about him," says Cat.
"Look at that sexy grin."

Nancy says, "They're just friends, or so I'm told.
Amy's dress is pink, and he has a pink cummerbund to
match."

"Everything is pink now," says Cat.

"Why don't Jack ever take anything in color?" Lila
asks. "I have to use my imagination."

"I guess that's the idea," says Nancy. She laughs. "Jack
didn't want to send this picture earlier, but I guess he
changed his mind. He thought you might have a fit over
the hair."

Smiling, Lila lays her glasses on the nightstand. "Well,
I'm mighty proud," she says. "You sure did put out a fine
youngun, and stayed married—for how long now?"

"Almost twenty years. It was twenty years ago
today—"

"Today?"

"No, not today. That's a song allusion. Not till this
fall."

"That's a record," Cat says in a flat tone.

Lila realizes the sadness in Cat's voice. She is certain Cat could have patched it up with Dan. Quickly, Lila says, with deep pride, "All of my children have given me some mighty fine grandchildren."

"Krystal and Scott both asked about you on the phone, Mom," Cat says. "Krystal hates it in Hopkinsville and wants to come home."

Nancy gathers up the photographs, promising to leave them for Lila to look at again later.

"Y'all don't have to be here every minute," Lila insists to Cat and Nancy.

"We're here because we care about you," says Cat.

"Well, you're showing it," Lila says. A sudden swell of emotion rises in her throat. The tugging sensation of nursing them as babies is as clear as yesterday. Nancy liked to bite. Cat was always hungry. Nancy wasn't weaned until she was two and a half. Rosie would say, "You're giving that youngun too much peezootie." That was a word of Rosie's Lila never heard anyone else use.

"Is there anything you want us to do?" Nancy asks.

With a little catch in her voice, Lila says, "There's something I wanted you to promise me. I didn't get to say it before."

They listen, like a pair of young cats fixed on a squirrel. Lila says, without her voice breaking, "I want you to take care of your daddy if something happens to me. He won't be able to take care of hisself."

"Don't worry, Mom. We'll take care of him." Cat caresses Lila's hand, picking at a cuticle where nail polish has smeared.

Lila says, "I don't want to be buried in that Spring Valley mausoleum. It's on the side of the road on a curve, and a truck could come along and bust it open."

"Don't think that way!" Nancy says.

Cat leans forward to give Lila a hug. "We'd never leave you by the side of the road. You know that."

"I wouldn't have found that knot if it hadn't been for you. In the old days, people didn't get breast cancer. Or they didn't know they had it. They just got sick and died."

"Well, science can do amazing things nowadays," Nancy says. "And the chemotherapy is going to work."

"You just don't realize how far we've come," says Lila, squeezing Nancy's hand.

"Yes, I do. I would have died at age ten of pneumonia if it hadn't been for penicillin."

Nancy always has an answer. But she seems not to realize she had survived pneumonia another time, when she was two. That was before penicillin. The memory jolts Lila.

"Times are better now," she insists to her daughters. "You don't know how good you've got it."

Nowadays, Lila thinks, young people expect to have everything right at the start. House and car, washer and dryer. They're not patient. When she worked at the clothing factory, she earned enough money to make life a little easier. In the few years she worked there, she bought a steam iron, an electric mixer, an electric stove, a set of steak knives, a dinette set. Spence never wanted her to go to work, but after Nancy started to school, and before Cat and Lee came along, the factory was hiring. Excitedly, Lila applied for the job, wearing a suit she had made. The hiring man admired her sewing and gave her the job. She sat at a large machine, stitching in collars or cuffing pants. She put on weight, sitting long hours on the high stool, but her arms grew strong from pushing and pulling the heavy suit material through her machine. The oiled wood floors were sticky with clumps of thread, and the air was stifling, despite the overhead fans. She carried her dinner—pimiento or tuna-fish sandwiches, with the lettuce wrapped separately; and sometimes a tomato, and salt and pepper folded in little pieces of waxed paper. She usually carried cake or cookies. On her breaks and lunch period, it was a deep pleasure to drink a cold, slippery bottle of Coca-Cola from the large cooler in the hallway. Lila loved the people, the talk that went on above the noise. She bragged on her child and listened to others brag on theirs; they swapped pictures and stories. The woman at the machine next to hers had asthma attacks from the wool dust in the air, and they had to carry her outside occasionally. A man working at the end of her row always entertained the hands with songs popular on the radio. She can still hear him singing "Slow Boat to China." Recently someone told her he had left his wife and died of a brain tumor in Arizona, alone. Another woman was always called "Miss Gregory" instead of her first name because she always dressed so elegantly for such rough work. They would say, "Miss Gregory sets on a pillow sewing a fine seam." Lila felt that way too, proud and alive. It was piecework, and sometimes she could make nearly ninety cents an hour, she was so fast.

Later, Cat has gone down the hall to the bathroom and Nancy is reading. Lila is telling Mrs. Wright she doesn't think her cancer has spread, when Cat returns, excited. "Did you see that prisoner on this floor? There's a guy with a guard from the state penitentiary. He's two rooms down the hall. He looks really sick, like he couldn't crawl an inch even if he tried to escape."

Lila shudders. "I hope that guard don't fall asleep. That's all I need, to be held hostage in the hospital!"

Mrs. Wright says, "It won't make me one bit of difference."

ELEVEN

On SUNDAY Lila's half-sister, Glenda, and her husband, Bill, stop by the hospital with a basket of artificial violets. It has a little ceramic rabbit in it, nibbling at the leaves. Lila is wearing her good blue gown and a bed jacket. Cat put Lila's makeup on her that morning and fixed her hair. Lila's scalp itches, but she doesn't want to wash her hair for fear of catching cold.

"Well, Lila, are you going to have to have cobalt?" Glenda asks. Glenda is overweight, with baby-fine light hair that used to be a pretty blond.

"No, I'm not," says Lila happily. "Just shots and pills for six months, and then they do all the tests again to see if it spread."

"I told Bill I didn't think you'd have to have cobalt," says Glenda.

Bill is a red-faced, deliberate sort of man, a retired farmer. He says defensively, "Well, seems like they want to put everybody through that."

"I don't think it spread very much," Lila says. "I could feel it in those leaders under my arms, but they think they got it all out." She runs her hand down her arm, which is stiffening up. The physical therapist has been there, instructing her how to work her arm. Lila has to grasp a yardstick, one hand on each end, and slowly raise it above her head, then lower it and swing it from side to side.

Glenda says, "We heard you're going to be operated on again, Lila."

Lila nods. "Depends on what they find out with my neck." She scrapes her fingers down her throat. "The blood ain't going through good."

Glenda says brightly, "Bob Barber had *his* veins cleaned out and he said it was like getting new glasses. He could think better after they operated."

"Are they going to do that test where they shoot you with the dye?" asks Bill.

"Uh-huh. I purely dread it too."

"They say that really hurts," Bill says. "They shoot it in your leg and it works its way up to your head and burns."

"They told me I had to lay real still for eight hours after they do it," Lila says. "If I turn over it might be dangerous."

"A clot might go to your brain," Glenda says.

"How have y'all been?" Lila asks, changing the subject. If Spence were here, he would be furious at them.

"All right, I reckon," says Glenda. "Bill here has to go in for his checkup—he has sugar—and he has to have tests for that spasmatic colon he's got."

Bill, hacking at a cough, says, "I told them I wasn't going to have that test where you drank that drank again. I had that last year, and my bowels backed up and didn't move for three months. It made a knot as big as my fist. It stayed there and everything went around it. I liked to died."

Glenda laughs. "He sure was something to live with while that was going on."

"Lila, you look like a spring chicken," says Bill. "Why, your hide won't hold you when you get home!" He offers to get Cokes for everyone.

"You can get a free drink in the lounge," Lila says.

After he leaves, Lila says, "I'm so proud to see you, Glenda!"

Glenda was eight and Lila was four when their mother died. Lila has one memory of her: a chubby little woman with dark hair, saying "fried pies" out on a porch, with a dog running up from a field—somewhere Lila could never identify. Her mother was only about twenty-eight when she died, of childbed fever. Glenda, who remembered her better, told Lila once, "She was light-complected and had pretty teeth. She liked to ride horses, and they say that's why she died. She rode a horse when she shouldn't have." The baby died too. Lila had been told it was a girl. Lila's father left Lila at Uncle Mose's and disappeared. Glenda went to live with her real daddy and his second wife in a little place down below Wolf Creek.

Lila didn't see Glenda again until after she married Spence and the war was over. Lila and Spence visited Glenda one Sunday afternoon. They sat on Glenda and Bill's porch and watched the traffic go by. Lila remembers her happiness that day—Glenda's daughter, Laura Jean, teaching Nancy how to ride a little red scooter; a dusty driveway; a setting hen; a can of sorghum Bill gave them. She remembers Glenda shooing flies from the apple slices spread out on a screen door to dry in the sun. Glenda was fat. That day she told Lila the baby their mother died with was a boy, not a girl.

"Lila, how are those daughters of yours treating you?" Glenda asks now.

"Oh, they've been awful good to me. They've been here every minute." Lila laughs. "They froze my corn the other evening. They should have done it in the morning when the dew's wet."

"It won't be crisp," Glenda says, nodding. "It'll be tough."

"I hope I'm out of here in time to do all the pickles. They'll draw the line at pickles."

"Nobody can do dill pickles like you can, Lila. You've got a secret recipe, I believe. One of these days I'm going to get you down and mash that recipe out of you."

"I just do it by guess. Last year I got them too sour. They was sour enough to make a pig squeal!" Lila laughs, then hiccups.

The old woman's voice booms through the curtain. "Who's got the he-cups over there?"

"Me," says Lila. She can't get comfortable, and the little jolts hurt her incision.

"You're a-growing," Mrs. Wright says. "That's what that means."

"I hope so," Lila says, pulling at her gown. "I wish I could grow a new jug."

"You can't get no sleep around here to save your neck," Mrs. Wright says. "They come in here late last night and started burning the house down!"

Lila sees the prisoner trudging past the door, clinging to his uniformed guard. His gown gapes open in the back, exposing his hairy rear end. He shuffles along, his head bent. Lila feels a sudden foreboding of death. This is all there is left to life: lying here in a hospital gown with her breast amputated, watching a bare-butt criminal go by and listening to a nutty old woman griping behind a curtain. Days ago, Lila told herself she was ready to go, that she had made her peace with the world, that she had had a good life and she was grateful. But now she revolts. She doesn't want to give up. She swings out of bed a little too quickly, and a pain shoots through her arm. But that's O.K. It will go away.

"Walk me down the hall," she says to Glenda. "I ain't ready to die yet."

[92]

TWELVE

"*Y*OU'RE NOT EATING for us, Mrs. Wright,"
the nurse says disapprovingly. This nurse is the cute one,
with the tiny feet. She's the only nurse who bothers to
chat with the old woman.

"She made a little sign on it," says Lila.

"I like broccoli cooked *done,*" says Mrs. Wright, sitting
up against her pillows defiantly and pushing her tray trol-
ley forward. "I like all kinds of greens. I could eat my
weight in asparagus. But not raw."

It's time for Lila to breathe oxygen. The nurse's aide
hauls the breathing contraption to Lila's bedside and pulls
the curtain between the beds. She aims the blue mask at
Lila's face.

"I believe my lungs is clearing up," Lila says to her.

"Well, they ought to be if you keep off them cigarettes," the girl says.

"Woman!" Mrs. Wright booms through the curtain. "I
did something for sixty-five years and then quit—and you
can too."

"What's that—smoking?" asks Lila.

"Naw—chewing tobacco. I started in the first grade,
but since I was operated on four days ago I haven't wanted
a chew. Got a bad taste in my mouth."

Lila can't reply because she is holding her breath. The
girl says, "You're doing good. Just hold it two more seconds. There."

Lila says, rubbing her neck, "These veins need oxygen."

"That smoking was closing them down," the girl says.

"I'm worried about that test they're going to run on my neck. They don't want to operate on both sides at once. They need to keep one vein open to feed the brain in case I have a stroke on the operating table." The words rush out. Lila can talk to the nurses about her fears, but doctors make her flustered.

"I'm sure they know what's best for you," the nurse's aide says. "Now breathe in again. The test will tell them which way to go."

"I'm more scared of that test than I am of the operation," Lila says. She sucks in air, feeling her face go red, her stitches tickling.

As the girl leaves, she rips open the curtain again, and Mrs. Wright says, "I'll be glad when I get back to my cat."

"Well, that's the first I heard you were going to leave the hospital!" says Lila. "I thought you wasn't aiming to leave here alive."

Mrs. Wright grumbles and works at her short-tailed gown, which has ridden up. "The doctor didn't say nothing about going home, but he said something about getting these belly steeples out. I feel like jerking 'em out myself. They put a screw in and some plastic. I had this herny for five or six years, and I was doing just fine with it till they started in bellyaching about it."

"Is somebody feeding your cat?" Lila misses Abraham. Spence won't give him enough attention.

Mrs. Wright shakes her head. "I guess she'll find something. That cat—she's a beautiful cat. Calico. She has the prettiest face. Where she's white she's *white,* and where she's black she's *black,* and where she's red she's *red!* She ain't got no tail. When she was a kitten she got in the hay baler and got her tail cut off. And she got her ears snipped off too somehow. She's crippled up in one paw. But she can catch mice. She catches 'em with one paw and stuffs 'em in her mouth and reaches out and hooks another one. That cat sleeps with me in the house every night in the world!"

"My cat doesn't come in the house," Lila says. "Spence never did like cats in the house."

"I'd tease the menfolks and offer 'em a chaw of tobacco straight out of the tobacco barn. I'd say you ain't a man if you can't chew that." Mrs. Wright laughs, a man's grunt. "If you chew tobacco, you won't never have worms. Lands, I ain't worked tobacco in ten years! That's how I ruptured myself, lifting a ten-by-twenty-five presser of tobacco."

"We never raised tobacco. I've got corn coming in and my girls don't know how to do it right."

"Honey, there ain't a soul to tend to my garden. I've got bell peppers and okry and Kentucky Wonders. Everything will ruin."

The TV news comes on, and the old woman says, "The politicians send all our money overseas, where all they do is fight and all they ever *will* do is fight."

The hospital routines are becoming too familiar—the florist's delivery cart passing by the door, the physical therapist who comes in each morning to help Lila work her arm to keep it from freezing up, the boy who sweeps the floors every afternoon, the night nurse with the cold hands and the way she has of popping the thermometer in Lila's mouth just as though she were using a dipstick to check the oil level in a car engine. When Lila asked the night nurse about the prisoner, she said, "I don't know what happened to him, but I sure wouldn't want to meet him in a dark alley."

Lila tries to read recipes in *Family Circle,* but her eyes blur and her glasses don't help. She would like to read from the Bible in the drawer of the nightstand, but the print is too fine. The preacher is supposed to come by, but he hasn't.

THIRTEEN

*S*ITTING IN THE LOUNGE while Lila naps, Spence is surrounded by worried-looking strangers, most of them overweight. Human beings come in such freakish forms, it always surprises him to be in a crowd of them. His nerves are bad. He can't sit still. Downstairs, he saw a woman in a wheelchair; evidently she was too fat to walk. She was the fattest woman he'd ever seen outside a circus. He works a Coke out of the ice in the cooler and lifts the tab. He takes a long drink and belches. Heartburn. The night before, it woke him up at two-thirty and he couldn't go back to sleep. His head whirled, catching memories of recent events until he was brought up to date, to the awful present. If Lila didn't make it through the second operation, her funeral could be as early as next weekend. In the dark, tossing in bed, he imagined her funeral. He couldn't stop whole scenes from playing in his head, like a TV documentary. The sermon, the flowers, perfunctory conversations with the kinfolks at the funeral home, coming home with his children and solemnly feasting on that food the neighbors brought.

If this is going to be her time, then what he and Lila should do is have a last fling together. But he can't go in her room and make love to her. He can't even talk to her or tell her how he feels while she's lying there in that white-cold bed with the nurses bumbling around the room like doodlebugs working on a cowpile. And now it seems likely that the doctors will get hold of her again, with their knives and scissors, probing violently in another place precious to him—her rugged throat, always tanned and healthy. The surgeons in masks will probably laugh and joke while they work, probably because they're making so much money. They must feel immense power, like presidents and TV executives. Spence's stomach turns over as a cloud of cigarette smoke fills the room. Someone switches the TV from a fishing show to the Nashville channel. Spence hates hillbilly music.

Lee and the kids came to see Lila earlier that afternoon. Now Lee joins Spence in the lounge, drinking a Sprite and gazing vacantly at the TV while Jennifer and Greg explore the hospital. Lee always seems tired. He didn't want to learn farming because he didn't want to get up at four to milk, but he has to work even harder at his factory job. He owes the bank almost four hundred dollars a month for a squatty little brick ranch house on a hundred-foot lot in town with no trees. It makes Spence sick.

The prisoner enters the lounge with the guard, who walks him around the room as if on an inspection tour. He is huge and young, with short blond hair and freckles. He looks as though he might have been a nice boy who turned bad. His dark eyes somehow don't fit his physique—a clue, Spence thinks, to why he turned bad. Something about his body isn't quite right. The sight of him is jarring. The guy has probably known that all his life, and the conflict made him mean. The criminal's I.V. rolls along with him like an obedient dog on a rope.

"I bet he got stabbed," Lee says. "All those prisoners want to do is cut on each other when they get the chance."

Spence says, "When the guard has to go to the bathroom, he chains that guy to the bed. I saw him."

"He don't look strong enough to get very far."

Spence asks, "How does she seem to you?"

"Mom? Oh, she's bearing up. She almost seems like her old self." Lee stares at his lap. "I feel terrible that we dragged her to Florida."

"She worries," Spence says. "She gets something in her head. Like that deal with you and Cat over the air conditioner."

"Mom didn't have anything to do with that."

Spence rubs his hands against his jeans. "I thought Cat give you that air conditioner."

"I told you how it was." Lee takes his time lighting a cigarette. "Cat said I could have the air conditioner, so I went and got it and installed it, and then she changed her mind and wanted it back, but I already had it in the window. I had to rework the frame to get it set right. It would have been easier for her to get a secondhand air conditioner than to fool with this one. She got mad because I wouldn't let her have it back."

"She claims she just meant to let you borrow it."

"She said I could have it, and I took her at her word."

Words. Lila's kinfolks deliberately tried to hurt her with words. They put him in a sour mood. And her friends chattered about diseases. Lila ate it up. His daughters embarrassed him. They even complained to the doctors about the hospital food, but the doctors had nothing to do with it. When Lila's first meal after surgery was a hamburger with pickles and potato chips, Nancy said it wasn't nutritious, especially for someone with carotid-artery disease. "A greasy old hamburger!" Nancy snapped at the doctor. Spence wanted to spank her. He can remember when he and Lila were courting, and they went out for hamburgers. A hamburger and Coke at Fred and Sue's Drive-in was the most delicious meal they had ever had. Even after they were married, they looked forward to going out for hamburgers almost as much as they looked forward to making love. His mother was stingy with meat and cooked the same plain grub day in and day out.

Lee is speaking to him about subdivisions. Lee brings up subdivisions about once a month, trying to convince Spence that since his land is close to town it will be worth something someday.

"Why don't you sell off some frontage and get a start on a development?" Lee asks.

"What would I want to do that for?"

"You're setting on a gold mine."

"Good. You can come over and dig in it."

"You could sell one lot and get enough to build a house on another lot and then sell it at a profit."

"Why didn't Joy come today?" Spence asks.

"She went to Mister Sun. Her and her sister go to the tanning booth every chance they get. I gave her a membership for her birthday." Lee stands to go, as Jennifer and Greg appear in the lounge. "I have to get home and finish paneling the den. The wallpaper's peeling off, and Joy's having a fit."

"You're going to do that on Sunday?" asks Spence, surprised. "I thought your mama taught you not to work on Sunday."

"I don't have time during the week, with overtime."

"Why don't you repaper? Ain't that cheaper?"

"No. I'd have to put up some new gypsum board, and by the time you get gypsum board and tape it and paint an undercoat, it's cheaper to panel." Lee clutches his Sprite can, crumpling it, left-handed.

"Paneling's got formaldehyde in it," says Spence. "It causes cancer. Ask Nancy. Nancy can explain it to you."

"Nancy's got an explanation for everything," Lee says

with a laugh. "What does she say caused Mom to get cancer?"

"Bacon grease. She says them veins in her neck is stopped up with bacon grease."

"Bacon grease in her neck?" asks Jennifer, Lee's seven-year-old.

"Come on, Goofus," says Lee to Greg, who is punching on Lee, trying to get his attention. "Let me know if there's anything I can do," Lee says to Spence.

After Lee leaves, Spence goes to check on Lila one more time before he heads home for the evening. He runs into Cat in the hall. She's wearing some kind of pink getup with a green-flowered ruffle at the bottom.

"Hi, kid," he says. "Where you been all day?"

"I went to the River Days Festival. They had a flea market and a fiddle contest."

"Fiddles ought to be outlawed."

"Why?"

"They make too much noise. The way they screak gives me a rigor."

She ignores him. "Did you see how pretty Mom looked? I fixed her hair and painted her fingernails this morning before her company came."

He nods. "You look pretty too. Except your ears look like some tobacco worms are sucking on 'em." Her earrings are fat and pale green and hang down past her chin line.

Cat slaps at his arm playfully. "I don't know how Mom put up with you all these years," she says.

"Where are you going?" he asks when Cat turns toward the elevator.

"I have a date to go out to eat."

"With that guy that took you up to Carbondale and left you that time?"

"No. He was a jerk."

"I thought you had more sense than that."

"Well, sometimes you just get in a fix and you don't know how you got there."

The elevator doors open and she steps on, waving goodbye. As the doors close, he remembers the time Cat was coming down the lane to meet him in the field. She was only about three. She crawled under the fence and started across the pasture toward him when a bull saw her and headed her way. "Go back, Cathy," he cried. "Get under the fence!" He never saw such a calm, smart child. She purposefully turned and sped toward the fence and crawled under. He was always proud of that, of how smart she was.

FOURTEEN

A WOMAN from the mastectomy support group arrives the next afternoon, bringing Lila a temporary pad to stuff in her brassiere until she can be measured for a permanent one. Lila feels embarrassed because both her daughters and Spence are right there. Spence is reading the newspaper noisily, rattling the pages and jerking them out smooth. Lila worries about his nerves.

"It's called a prosthesis," the woman explains. Lila did not catch her name. Cheerful and little, pert as a wren, she stands beside the bed, speaking to Lila like a schoolteacher. She presents Lila with the object, which is in a plastic bag.

"Law," says Lila. "That weighs a ton." It reminds her of those sandbags used to hold down temporary signs on the highway.

"I can tell you're surprised," the woman chirps. "We don't realize the weight we're carrying around. You can put a strain on your back if you don't get properly fitted. So don't just stuff your bra with any old thing to make it look right. It's got to feel right and it's got to be the right weight, or you can run into serious problems."

The woman says she has had a mastectomy herself, and presumably she is wearing one of these sandbags in her brassiere. Lila notices Spence squirming. Nancy and Cat don't jump on this woman the way they did on the doctors. Cat is playing solitaire and Nancy is reading a book. Mrs. Wright is asleep.

The woman tells a long tale about her own mastectomy. "I was worried about recurrence," she says. "And I did have a lump to come in the other breast. It was tested and it was benign, but I made the decision to have the second breast removed too. I just didn't want to take the chance of having cancer again. Now that may sound extreme to you, but it was just the way I felt. So I'm free from worry, and the prosthesis works just fine."

The woman's little points are as perky as her personality. If the originals were that small, she probably doesn't miss them, Lila thinks. The woman talks awhile about balance, and then she talks about understanding. She has a packet of materials for Lila to read. "You may get depressed over losing part of your femininity," she says. "And we want you to know we're available to help." Lila listens carefully, but she can't think of anything to say.

"The doctors were skeptical when we started our organization," the woman says, leaning toward Lila and speaking in a confidential half-whisper. "But after we advertised, we had fifty women come to the first meeting. There was a great need for this, and we want you to know that we're there to serve you."

"Would I have to come all the way to Paducah?"

"Yes. That's where we hold our meetings, on the first Monday night of each month."

"Well, I don't get out much at night. And I don't like to drive on that Paducah highway."

"Let me urge you just to try it and see what it does for you. I'll give you the names of some people to contact." She talks on and on, about how the family should be understanding. In the packet are letters to daughters and sons and husbands. Spence and the girls are pretending they aren't there. "The letters say things that you may be uncomfortable saying, things you might be afraid to say, but they will explain your feelings at this delicate time when you need emotional support. All you have to do is send the appropriate letter to your daughters and your husband and to your sons, if you have any. It will be a nice surprise for them if you just send them in the mail. It's a much easier way for you to communicate your feelings."

"My girls have stood by me," Lila says, nodding proudly at Cat and Nancy. "And my boy works long hours and can't come as often, but he does when he can. Nancy flew all the way down here from New York."

"Boston," Nancy says, peering over her reading glasses.

"That's the same thing to us down here," the woman says with an apologetic smile.

"How much will this thing cost?" Lila asks. "If you charge by the pound, it might be high." She laughs at herself. She wonders why the woman didn't replace her breasts with big ones. Small-breasted women were always envious of Lila.

"The important thing is to get the proper fitting. With your fitting, and the bra and the prosthesis, the package comes to about a hundred and fifty dollars."

"Good night!" Lila and Spence cry simultaneously.

"But it's an important investment."

After the woman has gone, Spence says, "Will Medicare cover that?"

"I doubt it," Lila says. "I failed to ask her. Law, I hope' I don't have to have false teeth anytime soon! I won't be able to keep track of that much stuff."

"You don't need that thing. We can rig you up something."

"Why, shoot, yes," Lila says. "I ain't spending a hundred and fifty dollars for a falsie."

Nancy laughs. "I read about a woman who stuffed her bra with buckshot, and she got stopped at the airport by the metal detector."

Cat says, "I heard about a woman who had an inflatable bra, and she went up in an airplane, and with the change in air pressure they exploded!"

They're all laughing, and Lila spontaneously tosses the prosthesis to Spence. "Catch!" she cries. Spence snatches it out of the air and flings it to Nancy and Nancy tosses it to Cat. Cat starts to throw it to Lila but stops herself, probably realizing Lila's right arm is weak. Lila is laughing so much her stitches hurt. Cat hands her the little sandbag and Lila says, "Well, it'll make a good pincushion."

They all laugh even harder then because Lila is in the habit of keeping stray straight pins and safety pins fastened to her blouse, and more than once in her life she has accidentally jabbed her breast with a pin.

FIFTEEN

"WELL, so long," says Lila to Mrs. Wright, who is riding out the door in a wheelchair. She's going home.

The old woman crouches, her eyes aimed at her belly. She's in a print dress, lavender and green. She doesn't look up, but grunts faintly. Lila hopes she never develops such an attitude.

"I bet she can't wait till she gets back to her trailer so she can fix her up a mess of hog jaws and turnip greens," she says to her friends Mattie and Eunice, who are visiting. "She wouldn't eat a bite here."

Mattie and Eunice are in Lila's card-playing group. Last year, Reba was the fourth, and this year the fourth is Addie Mae Smith. But now Addie Mae is visiting her daughter in Florida and doesn't know Lila is in the hospital. "The flowers are from all of us, though," Mattie says, giving Lila a bowl of houseplants. "Addie Mae can go in on them when she gets back."

"I had a big crowd Sunday," says Lila. "Cat fixed my hair, but the curl's fell out now." She tugs at some stray sprigs. Cat took such care with her, fluffing her hair expertly with the plastic pick, like a hen pecking fondly at her chicks. When Cat was fussing with her, she said, out of the blue, "Mom, I know I didn't do the right things the right way. I should have gone to college and not married so young. But everything's different now, and you don't know how hard it is to work it all out. Things aren't the way they used to be—if they ever *were.*" She sounded bitter, but then she said, "It's not your fault I didn't turn out right. You're the sweetest mother in the world, and I'll never be as good as you." They had cried together for a moment, until they were interrupted by a nurse with a blood-thinner shot.

Mattie and Eunice won't let Lila say anything bad about herself. They tell her how good she looks. They chatter about their families and events at church. The conversation works around to the weather occasionally, and that prompts them to tell her again how good she's looking. They bring her a nightgown—store-wrapped in pink flowered paper. Lila can tell that it won't hang right over her new bustline, but it's the thought that counts. Mattie and Eunice haven't mentioned her breast. No one mentions Reba and her months of suffering. It's as though Reba never existed. Lila folds the gown and places it inside the tissue in the box. She smooths out the wrapping paper and folds it to save.

"It's freezing in here," Mattie says.

"I've been cold as a frog," Lila says. "Nancy and Cat had to bring me an undershirt and this sweater." She has on a blue cardigan of Cat's. "In here, I can't tell what the weather is."

Mattie has to get up and stir for her circulation. She sets the gift box on a shelf in the closet. Restlessly, she pokes in Lila's things, while Eunice flips through one of Cat's magazines. Mattie pats her little gray curls, flashing her rainbow of rings. Her rings and brooches and beads overwhelm her small frame. She has a whole houseful of doodads she collects from yard sales, and she spends half her time dusting. Lila wouldn't have the patience.

Eunice is sitting close to the bed so Lila can see the

pictures in the magazine. Eunice pauses over a picture of a handsome young man in his underwear.

"Look at all that going to waste," Lila says to Eunice.

"Are you sure that ain't stuffing?" says Eunice, examining the picture carefully.

"No, that ain't stuffing! That's the real thing!"

Eunice begins giggling and then Lila starts. Her breast jiggles and pulls across at her stitches. Eunice's face is red.

"I'm liable to say anything," Lila says. "This place is making me goofy. The nurses think I'm nuts."

Mattie looks disapproving, but Lila loves to watch Eunice laugh at a sexy joke. Eunice is a widow. Her husband, Herbert Wall, was big and fat, and Eunice once said he had such a load of "equipment" that it gave him a hernia. That remark made Lila think of a sheep, its swinging sack the size of a mushmelon. The boy in the underwear ad is young enough to be Lila's grandson, but he makes her feel a twinge of desire. She wishes she could go home right now and get in bed with Spence. One of the magazines Cat brought mentioned that men lose their desire for women who have had mastectomies. The thought hurt her and made her feel an anxiety like the urges she used to feel when she was working tobacco and she first knew Spence. He lived five miles down the road, and he would walk past the field where she worked after school and dawdle there. Lila's uncle found out he was hanging around and tried to scare him away, but Spence was daresome and he flirted openly with her, slowing down her work. Whenever she broke a tobacco plant by mistake she buried it so Uncle Mose wouldn't find out. She used to meet Spence at the edge of the tobacco field, down in the creek. They chewed gum from the black gum tree. It made their teeth black and their breath fresh, and when they kissed it was like a cool, sweet breeze.

[109]

Mattie walks over to the bed and stares closely at Lila. "When are they going to operate on your neck?"

"I have that test tomorrow, and they'll operate a-Thursday, depending on what they find out." She closes her fist and opens it. It feels slightly numb.

"Are you scared, dear?" Eunice asks.

"I didn't have time to get scared the first operation, and now there's so much going on I can't think. My brain was addled anyway." Lila laughs. "Probably from being out in the hot sun."

"All that gardening you do, Lila," says Mattie kindly.

"I've never seen anybody do as much yard work as you do," says Eunice. "You've got a lot to be proud of. You've got the prettiest yard."

"Well, I sure am lucky, with my children, my family, the things I've done. All the trips I got to go on." Lila is growing sleepy. Her arm feels numb, the way it did in Florida.

"That's something to be thankful for, Lila," says Mattie, and Eunice nods.

"Spence would hate all the noise and waiting in line. He'd rather be home digging taters!" Lila laughs at the thought of Spence on a bus tour with the senior citizens. Abruptly, she says, "The doctor said I could live without a breast. He said I'd be surprised."

"My sister told me about a woman she works with who had her breast takened out," says Mattie, who has been standing by the crucifix on the wall, studying it as if it were for sale. "She was a terminal case. The cancer had spread to ninety percent of her lymp' nodes."

"It just spread to two of mine, but they takened them out," Lila says, touching her right armpit.

Mattie doesn't seem to hear Lila. She's wound up, like the musical doll Cat gave Lila once for Mother's Day. "But

[110]

come to find out—this woman lived!" Mattie continues. "She had chemotherapy five years and she had cobalt, but the cobalt burned a hole in her heart and gave her heart trouble, and so she had to have her chest wall replaced. She waited too late to sue, because her husband thought she was going to die and he didn't think they could do anything. But she got better and then all of a sudden her husband died of a brain tumor, and then six months after that her son was killed in a car wreck! But *she's* still a-kicking."

"I never heard of so many things happening to one woman," says Eunice.

"It's a miracle she bore up under all that," Lila says.

"Well, Lila, the Lord never gives us more than we can bear," says Mattie.

"Yes," Lila says, gazing at the underwear ad.

One summer night shortly before her eighteenth birthday, she ran away with Spence and they were married. She brought her few possessions in a bag she had sewed out of sacking. She didn't even have a Bible. They drove across the state line, not really knowing if they would go through with the plan. It seemed outrageous, like something the old folks told about in one of their stories of the pioneers. Spence promised her a good life. He already had a start, on his father's farm. "I don't ask for much," he said. "Just to have my clothes kept up and food on the table." He drove an old Ford with a door that rattled and headlights that sometimes blinked out. While searching for the justice of the peace, they got lost on a back road, which ended in a woods across from a corn-field. Spence persuaded her to have the honeymoon first and then look for the justice of the peace later, arguing that they'd never find this perfect, peaceful place again. Lila was always a practical person and she could see his line of reasoning. When they finally arrived at the justice of the peace, the man had already gone to bed, but he obligingly got up, tied his barking dog, and performed the service for them on his front porch. In the dim porch light, neither he nor his wife, who acted as the witness, in her curlers and housecoat, could tell how wrinkled Lila's clothes were. She had on a new suit she had made, with shoulder pads, and Spence told her she was the most beautiful girl in the world. They sneaked into his house before daylight, and at milking time he brought her out of his room to meet his astonished parents. She was tall and thin, but even then her breasts were large, and they jutted forward into the surprised line of sight of her new mother-in-law.

The artificial breast is in the drawer. The pamphlets are hard to read, and the letters don't say the right things—not the things she would say to her husband, her daughters, her son. The girls have read through the packet, and Lila thinks it would be even more embarrassing to send letters than to say what she felt. The letters wouldn't sound like her. One of the pamphlets says, "Women usually go through periods of depression after a mastectomy. They equate their femininity and their sexuality with the lost breast." Lila is so confused, with so many people telling her what to think, that she can't quite grasp her own thoughts.

Last week, the day she was operated on, she remembers waking up in a fog, wanting to turn over onto her side, but something held her flat. The room was extremely cold. Her feet were numb. And then she felt her habitual cough grab her and shake her out like a dust mop. She wondered, even then, before she was sure they had removed her breast, how they disposed of it: Did it all come out in one hunk, or did they hack it out? She thought about dressing a chicken, the way she cut out the extra fat and pulled out the entrails. She thought of how it was so easy to rip raw chicken breasts.

SIXTEEN

$\mathcal{B}$ILL BELTON's brick ranch house, just down the road from Spence, is only a few years old, but the plastic shutters are warped and one of the downspouts is crooked. In the backyard, a wash line runs between the house and Bill's dish antenna. The dish has a happy-face painted on it. Bill's tobacco barn sags, the paint worn off years ago. Bill hasn't grown tobacco since the bottom fell out of the burley market. Now he has a hundred acres in soybeans and a crop-dusting plane. Spence often sees Bill's plane above the countryside—flying low, aggravating cows and horses.

"Ho, there, Spence," says Bill, who is down by his dilapidated barn, working on his tractor. The airplane is parked under a makeshift carport shelter on the side of the barn.

"When do you aim to dust my beans?" asks Spence. "The grasshoppers is eating 'em up. In the middle of the night I can hear 'em gnawing. I'm afraid I'll wake up one morning and the fields will be bare."

"I been meaning to get over there, Spence," says Bill, picking up an oilcan from a rickety table of rusted tools.

The outside wall of the barn is decorated with squirrel tails, snakeskins, and a coon skin. Memories of dead animals jam Spence's mind: a butchered hog, a cat smashed under the car's tire, a crippled dog slowly dying of a fes-

[115]

tering wound, a cow that was down and had to be shot, a bird with a wing shot to shreds.

"How's Lila doing?" Bill asks.

"She's fussing at me, as usual." Spence grins. "But she's getting some tests done today, and I'm afraid she'll have to be operated on again tomorrow—this time on her neck." He touches his neck and can almost feel it being slashed.

"The one where they go in and clean out your veins?"

Spence nods.

"Seems like everybody and his dog's having that one. Is Medicare going to cover all that, Spence?"

Spence shakes his head worriedly. "I doubt it. I heard if it's cancer they won't pay it all."

"Well, at least you've got some benefits from driving that van for the school. Me, I don't got nothing. I was in a mess here while back when Mozelle had colon trouble." He toys with the oilcan, as if he has forgotten what he meant to do with it. "They come at me to the tune of three thousand dollars. And I already owed fifty thousand on this machinery."

"So how did you manage? How'd you buy that airplane?" A few years ago, Bill had splurged on his combine—soon after building his house.

Bill just gazes off over the barn roof at some blackbirds wheeling around in the sky. Nothing but blackbirds swarm over anymore, Spence has noticed. Most of the songbirds have disappeared since the industrial park was built. Bill says, "You want some coffee, Spence? Want to come on in the house? Mozelle's gone to get her hair fixed, but I think I know how to run that coffee machine."

"No, I ain't got time. And coffee jags me out." Spence doesn't want to start in on his coffee spiel, about imports

[117]

versus domestic crops. He thinks the coffee habit is a conspiracy—to get people addicted to a luxury that comes from a foreign country.

"Since when do you drink coffee?" asks Spence as they walk toward the car.

Bill shrugs. "I got to be nearly this old before I found out it can keep you awake when you need to be awake. All that business about how you don't need as much sleep when you get old ain't true. It was just a story they told." He opens the screen to the porch and says, "Come on indoors. I want to show you something."

Bill's den wall is covered with what Spence calls "gimme caps"—caps with ads on them. Massey-Ferguson, Budweiser, John Deere, Black & Decker, Strong Feed Co. The wall is full of colors, reminding Spence of a game at a carnival where you throw darts at a wall of balloons. Bill shows Spence a green cap that says, "Hickman County Stud." Bill laughs. "A guy had this made up special for me, just for a joke."

Bill takes out a coffee can from a cabinet under the TV set. Spence remembers the rusty coffee-can lid that Lee stepped on when he was little. He was running in the grass and cut his foot open. Nancy panicked. She ran to the house packing him in her arms, her words streaming out incoherently, like the blood from Lee's foot. Nancy panics easily; that's why she thinks the world is going to be ruined by poisons and nuclear bombs and fat, anything she hears on the news.

"I don't want no coffee," Spence says.

"Hold your horses, Spence. This ain't coffee." Bill removes the plastic top from the can and pulls out a handful of pale, round seeds—like mustard seeds. "I'll sell you these babies for ten dollars a teaspoon," he says.

"Where'd you get those?" Spence knows what they

are—marijuana seeds. He recognizes them from something he has seen on TV.

"A guy gave 'em to me and I planted some of them." Bill dribbles the seeds back into the can. "You know how many I set out last year?"

"How would I know? I don't come over and count your crops."

"Twenty. Guess what I made off of 'em."

"I don't know. A thousand dollars?" Spence always exaggerates guesses like this to undercut the other guy's joke.

Bill laughs. "I set out about twenty slips, back in the cornfield. I had twenty acres in corn last year, so I strewed 'em out." He flings his arm toward his south fields. "These things grow like weeds, but you need to water 'em good. They need a lot of water the first two weeks. After that, they just grow like burdock. They do better if you sucker 'em. At the end of the summer, when they started turning, I cut the stalks off and packed 'em to the barn in a gunnysack and cured 'em. Then I put 'em in a big bed sheet and rolled it with a rolling pin and pounded the stalks good. I didn't want to take a chance on losing a smidgen of that leaf. Then I took the stalks out and packaged up the leaves in those little plastic zipper bags. And I took 'em up to the truck stop in Newton and sold 'em to a fellow I know. Them suckers brought twenty thousand dollars."

"Gah!" says Spence, his mouth open.

"A thousand bucks *apiece*, Spence." He shook the coffee can. "Look at these babies," he says gleefully. "My millions."

"Pretty soon you'll be sowing an acre of this stuff and then you'll get caught."

"Hell, Spence, I ain't talking acres. This is the small farmer you're talking to. I ain't no goddamn corporation."

Spence turns to go, and Bill says, "I figure there ain't nothing wrong with it. I don't sell it to kids."

"Yeah, but you sold it to truckers, and then they get out on the road, high on dope."

"Nah! They take it home. It ain't like tobacco, Spence. You don't smoke it all the time. You wait till you're setting around watching television or something."

"Sounds like you know what you're talking about."

"I'm just being a good farmer, Spence. Knowing my product. Now I'm ahead on my payments and I've got that airplane that can pull in the cash."

"Then I reckon you can give me a cut rate."

Bill grins. "For you, Spence, good buddy. I'll come early in the morning if it ain't windy. Better fasten up your calves tonight." He returns the coffee can to the cabinet under the TV. Jokingly, he says, "Why don't we go sow some of these seeds up along the railroad track?"

"I don't have time to get involved in organized crime," Spence says with a grin.

"You know what, Spence? You ought to go take a walk back to your back fencerow and see what's growing there."

"Why?"

"Those boys on the old Folsom place are liable to be growing something on your side of the line and you not know it. And then if the law was to find out—why, it's on your property, not theirs."

"I hadn't thought of that," Spence says, alarmed. "You reckon?"

"I wouldn't put it past 'em. They've got that new truck and I didn't see soybeans doing that good last year, and they've got that combine to pay for and they had a new pond bulldozed. They're really turning it on over there."

The Frost brothers—a bachelor and a widower—

bought out the old Folsom farm, the property behind Spence's, but they don't know how to farm it. They came from down in Mississippi and aren't used to Kentucky soil. Lila was upset with them once for running over her petunias when they came to bring some firewood from a dead post-oak tree they had sawed down on the fence line. Spence was surprised they had let him have the wood.

As Spence opens his car door, Bill calls after him, "Let me take you up for a ride in the airplane, Spence."

"I don't even like to ride in your truck with you, Bill. You're too reckless."

"Got to live dangerously, Spence!"

"Well, you seem to be doing that. You'll get cancer breathing them bug-killer fumes."

"Oh, go up with me sometime just for a ride. We don't have to spray when we go. I'll show you what your place looks like from the air."

Spence starts up his Rabbit. He would like to fly. He wishes he could just get in that flimsy little plane and fly off somewhere.

SEVENTEEN

*S*PENCE hates the familiar smells, the cold temperature, the sounds of the scurrying nurses. The sight of the old people being led for their walks down the corridor bothers him most. They clutch pillows to hold their insides in.

That morning Lila had the test she dreaded, and now she has to lie quietly all day, without turning or raising her legs. "It wasn't as bad as they said it would be," she says when Spence comes in. "It felt warm in my head, like it was going to blow up, but it didn't hurt that awful much."

"All that worry for nothing," he says, squeezing her hand. "That's the way you always do. You listen to them old women talk."

"The doctor says he wants to operate on the left side."

"Tomorrow?"

"Tomorrow about one o'clock." Her new roommate is staggering out the door with a nurse. "She had her gall bladder takened out," Lila explains to Spence.

"Where's the girls?"

"Cat had to go to work and Nancy's gone to see about the garden. Didn't you pass her on the road?"

"I didn't notice." Nancy has been driving Lila's car, even though the muffler is growing louder.

"All those machines they've got in the basement for the tests—it was the space age down there! I felt like I was on television, with all those gadgets they used." Lila shivers. "I'm taking cold. They tried to tell me they keep it cold to keep the germs down, but I always take cold when my neck gets chilled."

Her hand works away from his and grabs at the air. "Reach me some water," she says.

He pours water from her water jug into a paper cup and holds it close to her face. She can't raise her head and he has to bend the flexi-neck straw and aim it at her mouth. This is the extent of his ability to deal with the sick.

She says, "If I don't make it, I don't want to be stuck in that mausoleum. A truck could come along and bust that thing open."

"Don't worry about that," Spence says with a grin. "We'll put you back in the field where you can keep an eye on the corn crop."

She starts to laugh and is stopped by her cough. A pretty but snaggletoothed nurse materializes beside the bed. "How are we doing?" she asks.

"We're doing fine," says Spence.

"Let me sleep," Lila says. "I've had enough torture for one day."

"Honey, I just have to check one thing," the nurse says.

"Won't y'all ever leave me alone?"

"You're being so good we just don't want to let you go home," says the nurse cheerfully. "We're just trying to keep you here 'cause we like you so much. Sir, would you step outside?"

Spence waits in the hall, lost in a memory of Lila feeding a calf formula from a bucket with a nipple. The cow, Honey Bunch, had calved down near the creek, below the pond. When Spence brought the calf to the barn, the cow tagged along, nudging his elbow, making soft noises. The next day, Lila noticed her returning to the creek, confused. Lila followed her and found a second calf there, nestled beneath a hickory tree on the creek bank, too weak to follow its mother to the house. Lila said the cow had strained her milk by running back to the creek, trying to nurse both calves. Patiently, Lila hand-fed the calves and talked to them, even getting up in the night to go to the barn to tend them. She would do the same with wild rabbits, kittens, anything. Spence feels helpless. What if he had to feed her? Change her bed?

The surgeon arrives, in his green garb. Spence is relieved that Cat and Nancy aren't there to pounce on him.

"We have the results of the angiogram," the doctor says, glancing at his clipboard. "She's sixty percent blocked on the left side and forty percent on the other one. My recommendation is to open up that artery on the left side and pull out that plaque, and then see how she does. I don't want to do them both at once because of her weakened condition. And there's a chance she'll do so well she won't need the other one done."

The thought of opening an artery makes Spence picture skinning a snake. He tries to think of what to ask. "She complained about that dizziness down in Florida," he says.

"The blood flow was impaired," the doctor says. He has a complexion like canned wienies and seems as delicate as a woman. He says, "We have to be careful removing the plaque, because if a fragment gets into the bloodstream it could flow to the brain and cause damage. And of course the angiogram doesn't show us everything. It doesn't show if there's blockage around her heart, for example."

Nancy and Cat would have thrown questions at him about her heart, but Spence doesn't want to ask about that. He says goodbye to the doctor, sees that Lila is trying to sleep, and leaves the hospital, glad to be out in the hot July sun. He spends the afternoon running errands—picking up bulk feed from the feed mill, paying the electric bill, gassing up his Rabbit. He has that coupon for the free tune-up, but the line at the gas station is too long, and he'd rather do it himself anyway.

When he gets home, Nancy is there, bringing a bucket of cucumbers and tomatoes from the garden. She's in shorts and a T-shirt, looking sixteen. He remembers her at that age, sitting on the corn planter behind him as he drove the tractor. She complained because she got so bored, sitting there all day in order to close up the seed bins at the end of each row while he turned the tractor. As they worked, she kept coming up with schemes for mechanical inventions to eliminate her job. "You're just not paying attention," he insisted to her. "There's everything here if you just notice." Weeds, the patterns of the rows, the language of the birds overhead, moisture levels inside the soil the harrow turned up. He felt free on his tractor. He could ride a tractor from now to the end of the world, rejoicing in the pleasure of his independence.

Now Nancy sets the bucket under a shade tree and he tells her what the doctor said.

"I know," she says, pulling her long bangs out of her eyes. "I talked to him before I left."

"The test wasn't as bad as she expected."

"No. She was scared of it, but it wasn't bad."

Indoors, he changes clothes and puts on his boots. He can't get used to keeping his clothes in the bedroom, instead of near the door, where they were handy.

"Where are you going?" she asks when he goes out again.

"Back in the field."

"I'll come with you."

They walk down the lane to the pond, Oscar bounding ahead, then occasionally racing back. Abraham follows them, his fluffy tail held high. At the pond, the ducks swim away from Oscar. Spence stoops to pet Abraham's head, but he slinks away from him and leaps into the soybeans after a grasshopper. The grasshoppers are jumping among the beans like giddy children on trampolines.

"Mom really loves that cat," says Nancy, who is playing with a sprig of dried grass, trying to get Abraham interested.

Spence says, "Do you know what old Cousin Dulcie said to Lila?"

"No, what?"

"She told Lila about some woman who had that operation and then went home and died."

"Dulcie has the sensitivity of a turnip."

Spence nods. "Do you think she's too weak to go through with another operation?"

"I don't know. She was always so strong it's hard to tell."

"Oscar!" Spence calls. The dog is onto a trail, his nose to the ground. "Oscar, don't you go scaring up them rabbits."

Nancy says, "Mom doesn't want us to think she's not strong and positive. It's her maternal instinct. She can't stop protecting us, even when she has been violated in the worst way—" She breaks off, as if she thinks Spence might not understand her words. He's embarrassed. She tosses the sprig of grass toward the pond and the ducks look up. "Is the water O.K. now?" she asks.

When the tobacco warehouse up on the highway caught fire last fall, the blackened, tar-stained water from the fire hoses ran down into the creek and emptied into the pond. The water was hot, and the heat killed the fish. The tobacco company official who investigated assured them the tar was harmless and offered them two thousand dollars compensation. It was twice as much money as they had invested bulldozing and stocking the pond, so they had to accept it, but Spence and Lila grieved, seeing the fish floating in the water, then massing on the bank. They had to bury them.

"It seems all right now," he says. "When it happened, the frogs was as thick as them grasshoppers on the beans out here. So all the frogs died, and all the fish. I even found a big mud turtle in with all them fish."

"Did you have the water tested?"

He shakes his head no. "It's O.K. There's a runoff, and the water keeps running in from the creek."

He can feel Nancy tense up, wanting to lecture him on how he should have sued. But Spence doesn't trust lawyers any more than he trusts the company officials. The two thousand was a good deal. Kicking at a shampoo bottle that has washed out of the creek, he says, "She's worried herself sick over first one thing and then another. The pond and losing them fish. And she worries about Cat being by herself at night and what it's doing to the kids. And then that business with Cat and Lee."

"I think Cat's sorry about that," Nancy says.

"Have you talked to her about it?"

"Not much."

"Have you seen Lee?"

"A couple of times, but we didn't talk about it. Cat was mad at Lee for taking Mom to Florida when she wasn't feeling well."

I can't live without Lila, Spence thinks suddenly. Somewhere from the depths of his memory sprouts an old scene of her milking a cow named Turnipseed. The flies

were bad. Lila tied Turnipseed's tail to the stanchion to keep it from switching her in the face as she milked. He can even remember the polka-dotted dress she was wearing on that particular day. There she is, sitting on the milk stool, splotches of lime on her heavy brown shoes. When the cows were all milked and turned out, she scraped the manure off the floor and scattered lime all over the concrete. That scene happened thousands of times; it is strange that one stands out—Turnipseed's tail, the spots on her shoes like the dots on the dress.

"What's going to happen to this farm?" Nancy is asking.

Spence is struck by how old he is, so old even his children are aging. "I'll leave it for you kids to fight over," he says. "I can't keep up this place much longer—I'm about give out. I can't keep the gullies filled up. The whole farm's going to wash away if I don't keep at it."

"It'll become a subdivision like that monstrosity down the road," Nancy says. "It makes me sad that we can't carry it on."

"Well, we had two strikes against us," Spence says. "Starting out with two girls." He grins at her, imagining Nancy as a farm wife instead of an adventurer.

"Why didn't you teach Lee how to farm?" she asks. "It's a shame he has to work such long hours at that factory."

"He makes a better living at what he's doing than he ever would on a farm these days."

"It still would have been good for him to know," Nancy argues. Back when she was in college, she would have argued the opposite. He remembers a time when she tried to persuade them to move to town and open a grocery store.

"I always made good, and we never had to do without," Spence says. "But nowadays a young couple would have to borrow too much to start out. There wouldn't be a living in it anymore—not in a place this size."

They head down the lane into the creek below the pond. A gap in the bank is stopped up with layers of rusted car parts, old bedsprings, chair frames—all filled in with piles of leaves. An enamel coffeepot and some rubber tubing have washed out of the trash. Oscar paddles in the creek, slopping his big paws through the shallow puddles. Nancy skips across on some flat rocks and Spence strides right through the mud and gravel. On the other side, Nancy stops and turns to face Spence.

"Daddy, do you remember one day when we rode the hay wagon across the creek? You were driving the tractor and Mom and I rode on top of the hay all the way back to the house."

Spence shook his head. "We did that every year."

"It felt like riding an elephant when the wagon bobbed down into the creek. Granny sent back our dinner at noon and we ate on the creek bank at the back field. She sent fried chicken and biscuits and ham and those white peas I like and slaw and sliced tomatoes and onions and a jug of iced tea."

"How do you remember all that?"

"I don't know. I just remember being happy that day."

A car horn sounds in the driveway, across the field. "That's Cat," Nancy says. "We've got to do corn again." But she doesn't leave immediately. She says, "That day Mom was so pretty. It was before she got worn down taking care of Granny. I thought then that she'd live forever." Nancy, suddenly fighting back tears, says, "When I was little, I don't think it ever once occurred to me that I might lose one of you."

Spence is too choked up to speak. Nancy crosses the

flat rocks again, her shoe sinking into some soft gravel, and when she reaches the other side, she says, "Cat came back here that day with the hired hand and the dinner, and she rode back with us. I remember that now. We found a bird's nest in a cedar tree, and down in the creek we saw some footprints of a raccoon. Cat tore her dress on the fence and cried. That was the summer you bought me a cowboy hat."

Nancy leaves, following the path along the upper creek, which feeds the pond. He's not sure he remembers that day, but he can see Lila riding on top of the load of hay as clearly in his imagination as he could in memory. Lila and the girls in straw hats, Lila in some of his old pants and a long-sleeved shirt with a rip in the sleeve. As the picture grows clearer in his mind, Nancy's straw hat changes to a cowboy hat, Cat's dress to a robin's-egg blue—the same as her car in the driveway now. He smiles, remembering the cowboy hat. He had to hunt all over town to find one Nancy's size.

He follows the creek line down toward the back fields. In the center of one of the middle fields is a rise with a large, brooding old oak tree surrounded by a thicket of blackberry briers. From the rise, he looks out over his place. This is it. This is all there is in the world—it contains everything there is to know or possess, yet everywhere people are knocking their brains out trying to find something different, something better. His kids all scattered, looking for it. Everyone always wants a way out of something like this, but what he has here is the main thing there is—just the way things grow and die, the way the sun comes up and goes down every day. These are the facts of life. They are so simple they are almost impossible to grasp. It's like looking up at the stars at night, seeing them strung out like seed corn, sprinkled randomly across the sky. Stars seem simple, even monotonous, because there's no way to understand them. The ocean was like that too, blank and deep and easy.

Spence moves on. Above, a jet plane flies over, leaving a white scar. At the back of the farm the creek joins another creek, a twisted gully that cuts through several farms before joining Wolf Creek. Oscar has strayed momentarily, but comes rushing up to lap at the water in the creek. The water is very clear, the pebbles shining. It is rarely deeper than Spence's knees, and in summer it is just patchy puddles, but sometimes Spence has dreams about swimming in this clear, shallow water. He dreams of the knock and dash of waves high as buildings.

The back field holds the ten acres of corn. It's tall, and the ears are fattening up. Oscar threads his way through the rows of corn, and Spence follows the narrow edge next to the fencerow. He reaches the back line just as Oscar rouses a cottontail, which bounds erratically along the path, then disappears into the blackberry briers. Perplexed, Oscar roots around, then gives up, coming to Spence as if to win approval for his restraint.

"Oscar, you know I don't want you catching them rabbits."

In Spence's opinion, dogs and cats should have amusing, old-fashioned names—Buford, Brutus, Nebuchadnezzar, Abraham. He doesn't like names like Fluffy and Fifi or names from television, like Mr. T. He knows a man with two Boston bull terriers named Cagney and Lacey. Spence never watches that show because Lacey's New York accent grates on his nerves.

There they are. It is true. A scattering of marijuana plants, thriving on the fertilizer he used on his corn. The plants grow in amongst the cornstalks of the first three rows, like inseparable companions. He wouldn't have guessed what pretty plants they are. The lacy leaves are almost tropical, like the vegetation he vaguely recalls from the islands in the Pacific. These plants are strong, with the unmistakable nature of weeds—hardy, tenacious, stubborn.

He counts thirteen of the plants. He suspects Bill knows about them, because it is odd that Bill mentioned the possibility. Bill's land joins Spence's on one edge, across the creek. Spence figures that Bill, not the Frost boys, planted them himself and decided to let Spence in on the joke, before Spence either got in trouble or missed out on the harvest. Bill and Spence have always played tricks on each other. Once some puppies showed up at the house. They had been dropped on the road. But Spence recognized the puppies—a litter from Bill's hound. Spence packed up the puppies in a box and dropped them back at Bill's house. The next time he saw Bill, the subject of the puppies didn't come up.

Lila often teased Spence about the way his pranks sometimes backfired—such as the time he got his eyes tested, part of the physical exam he had to take in order to drive the school van. The doctor positioned him in the chair but then left the room and jabbered with another patient about some designer glasses frames for such a long time that Spence grew irritated. He walked over to the eye chart across the room and memorized the last line, the finest print. Later, during the eye examination, Spence reeled off the last line. "That's amazing," the eye doctor said. "Read that again." Spence repeated the line of meaningless letters. "That's truly amazing," the eye doctor said. "For a man your age! Now, let's see you read it backwards."

A sound in the creek startles him. It's just a bird squabble. A blue jay soars out of a scaly-bark hickory. Spence gazes back over the field, taking in where he has been.

He can visualize that battle he was in as clearly as if it's happening now. He was below deck, frantically passing the five-inch shells to the main guns above, and then he could hear the one-point-ones—the dive-bombers were closer, heading for the capital ships. He could hear the antiaircraft guns going faster, sharper, the boom-boom-boom overlaid with bah-bah-bah-bop, then the rat-tat-tat chatter of machine guns. Sailors who had been on duty above deck told him later that radar had picked up six Japanese dive-bombers heading toward the carrier. The fleet shot down three of them, but the other three were closing in on their target. Suddenly several American fighter planes appeared, to finish up the job the ships failed to do. Like sparrows teasing a hawk, the fighters began swirling up and down and over and around each of the bombers. They shot down two of them, but the remaining bomber penetrated the defenses and was closing in on the big ship. The fighters swirled in all directions and then one fighter got on the bomber's tail, in the right position to shoot it down. The Japanese plane was already swooping toward the carrier, and the American fighter flew straight at him, like a mad bumblebee. Instead of shooting him down, the fighter rammed him from above and behind, just as crazily and fearlessly as the kamikazes nose-dived into the American decks. The explosion sent both planes cartwheeling, on fire, into the sea. It was impossible to believe, the crew said. He flew right up the Jap's ass. His guns must have jammed. They were sure his guns jammed, and there were just a couple of seconds to go before the enemy plane would have released the bomb. The fighter, in position, made an on-the-spot decision to die, to save the carrier. It was a moment frozen forever. The sailors talked about it all the way to Guam. They knew their ship might have to do something like that. At any moment their captain could whip the ship into the path of a torpedo. They might have to take a torpedo, the same way that fighter rammed the bomber. That's what they were there for.

Spence was sure the pilot's name would be in all the books he read later, but he couldn't find it. He was just another anonymous hero.

EIGHTEEN

*H*ER HEAD is clearing and she can turn over now and stir her limbs. She feels warmer. It is night, and a glow from the hall shines on the crucifix, highlighting it like a Christmas display.

The woman in the other bed has four visitors. Her family has paraded past the foot of Lila's bed all day: kids of all ages, uncles, aunts, parents, in-laws. The smallest child, the patient's little boy, seems to feel neglected and confused by his mother's illness. He slams the plastic bedpan on the bathroom floor deliberately, and when he's scolded he bursts into tears and says everybody's picking on him. His aunt takes his side. Lila would hate to have to cook for that bunch. They seem helpless without the woman at home to take care of them. They had gone to eat at the Cracker Barrel, reporting back to the sick woman every single thing they ate and how much it cost. Several times they got a laugh out of how the oldest boy spilled iced tea in his pie and ruined it. The little boy's grandmother said she had to cut up his ham for him and then he refused to eat it. She said she hated to waste ham, hogs were so high. The woman in bed is barely awake after her surgery, and the kinfolks are talking, talking, talking, laughing, telling stories. The noise competes with the television. Lila tries to watch *Family Feud,* but she has *Family Feud* right here, live.

She might die tomorrow.

Spence left soon after they brought her supper—broth and Jell-O and coffee, the same meal she had the night before her mastectomy. She didn't drink the coffee. When he left, abruptly, she felt so much was left unsaid. Lee and Joy and their children were there, as well as the crowd by the other bed, and Lila knew Spence's nerves couldn't bear the commotion for long. She imagined him going home, feeding the calves and the ducks, talking to Oscar, fixing some cereal, maybe eating a tomato, watching TV all evening—mumbling to himself the way he had started doing the last few years. She imagined that routine continuing. Tonight, tomorrow night, more nights, alone, for years.

When Spence's father died, Lila and Spence had talked about what each would do if the other went first. Spence was only fifty then, but he said he had just realized he would die someday, had never believed it before. But Amp was so old. His passing seemed natural. Much later, after Rosie had gone too, and Spence and Lila were alone together for the first time in their marriage, they felt as though they would live forever. They could never imagine one of them without the other.

If Spence went first, her life would change as much as it changed when she was eighteen and married him. She would be afraid to stay on the farm alone, with all the crime spreading out from town into the country these days. But she wouldn't want to have to move in with Cat or Lee and be a burden to them, the way Rosie was to her. Rosie lived on for ten years after Amp died, moving in with Spence and Lila toward the end. She was unhappy in their house. She would get up from a nap in the afternoon and eat breakfast, swearing the sun came up at three-thirty that morning. She thought the people on TV were in the room with them. "I want to go home," she'd say repeatedly, and sometimes she would go back, wandering up to the old house in her gown. But strangers lived in her house; they had rented the place. One night it burned down—a cigarette on the couch. After that, Rosie gave up her sewing and spent her days playing with scraps of material and pieces of paper, sorting them in boxes like a half-witted child. When she died, Lila found boxes and boxes of nothing but smaller boxes, and plastic bags stuffed with more bags and twist ties. She found strings and a lifetime's collection of greeting cards. Rosie even saved name tags from Christmas in a hosiery box. To Granny from Catherine. To Granddaddy from Lee.

Lila can't sleep. Random scenes pass before her eyes. The strong, comfortable smells of cows in the barn waiting to be milked, the steamy air in winter. Gathering in tomatoes before a frost. Sprinkling lime on the potatoes spread out on the ground in a stall of the barn. Laying the onions on screen-door racks above. An electrical storm scattering black tree limbs across the yard. Rosie's foot clamping down on the step-pedal of her slop bucket. Life has turned out so differently from anything she could have imagined at Uncle Mose's. The world has changed so much: cars, airplanes, television. She can't complain. She tries to go along with anything new, but she is afraid that inside she hasn't changed at all. It still hurts her to see liquor kept in a house where there are children, to see farmers out spreading manure on their fields on Sundays, to see young people fall away from the church.

Her innocence has always embarrassed her. Her children went away and came back with such strange knowledge she can't fathom. Nancy makes her feel dumb, with that bossy way she's always had of bringing home new ideas—cholesterol, women's rights. What Nancy knows is from books, but Cat knows people. She knows instinctively what looks good on her customers and knows how

[139]

to compliment them. Cat can make people feel beautiful. But Cat would rather spend money on expensive outfits than take the time to sew. Cat is never satisfied. Lila always says, "The more you get, the more you want." Lila never wanted much. But on Waikiki Beach, she felt thrilled and grateful for the chance to see what was out there. And she thought she would never get enough. She was seeing what Spence saw in the Navy, and maybe seeing what Nancy was looking for when she left home.

Growing into old age toward death is like shifting gears in a car; now she's going into high gear, plowing out onto one of those interstates, racing into the future, where all her complicated thoughts that she has never been able to express will be clear and understandable. Her mind cannot grasp these thoughts exactly, but there is something important about movement that she wants to tell. The way corn will shoot up after a rain. The way a baby chicken's feathers start showing. The way a pair of wrens will worry and worry with a pile of sticks, determined that the place they have chosen is the right one for a nest—the ledge over the door that gets disturbed every morning at milking time, or a pocket in a pair of overalls hanging on the wash line. A baby's tooth appearing like a shining jewel.

When her children were babies, Lila used to powder their bottoms and then kiss them right between the legs before she pinned on the diapers. They would squeal with pleasure. Nancy saw her do that to Cat and Lee when they were babies, and she was appalled. Lila said, "You don't see how I can do that, do you?" It was such overwhelming, simple love, there was nothing wrong with it. As they grew bigger and bigger, Lila couldn't tear herself away from them. She always wanted to pet them, though it embarrassed them. Even now she likes to kiss them on their lips. Lee turns red. Nancy is stiff, Cat more receptive. Cat is more like Lila, with the need to keep hugging her children, touching and holding.

After Spence came home from the Navy and began to build up the dairy again, they were happy, beginning to get a little ahead. One morning Spence had gone into town to deliver the milk and Lila was scrubbing overalls on the washboard out in the wash house. Rosie was adding coal to the fire under the wash kettle. Suddenly they heard Nancy crying indoors. When Lila rushed up the steps to the porch and to the kitchen to see if Nancy had fallen, she found Amp with the razor strop, whipping Nancy on the legs. Lila screamed at him to stop, but he kept on, aiming the strop precisely and fiercely. Nancy was howling, her legs already black with bruises. Like someone rushing into a jump-rope game, Lila ran through the flailing razor strop and snatched up Nancy, fleeing with her to their bedroom. "She climbed up on the table after I told her not to," Amp explained, following them. "She wouldn't *mind.* She has to learn to mind."

"Don't you never do that again!" Lila shouted. Her rage against his authority shocked her. She slammed the door and clung to Nancy on the bed, both of them crying until Nancy's sobs finally subsided into hiccups. Lila bathed the poor legs in Epsom salts, soaking the bruises. When Spence found out, he threatened his father, saying he would leave the farm, leave him without any hands to work it. But Spence was immobilized. There was nowhere to go, no way to get their own land. Lila doesn't believe Nancy remembers. She always loved her grandfather, and he never hurt her again. But she always clung to Lila for protection. Strangers frightened her, and she would look up at Lila, waiting for her mother to speak for her. Lila felt like an old mother hen holding out her wing. Even now,

Nancy's strange, frightened expressions remind Lila of that incident, and she doesn't have the heart to bring it up again. She never understood why Amp did that to Nancy. Men, Lila believed, had a secret, awful power. She was always taught not to hang around the men when they got together, when one came to visit and they would talk out at the stable. Rosie cautioned her about that.

A nurse interrupts Lila's thoughts, bringing her a pill. Lila doesn't ask what it is. She swallows it with a sip of water. The new roommate is getting some kind of midnight treatment, and she gives out a burst of little pup yelps.

There are loose ends: things Lila can't get out of her mind. The yellow bushes by the house that would bloom so pretty in the spring, with their sweeping arms. Spence cut them back so he could paint the side of the house and they grew bigger the next year, even more beautiful. Eventually, they died back, and for many years Lila longed to see those bushes again, but they were in the past. As you grow older, you give up things, hand things over to the younger generation. You plant a smaller garden. Instead of accumulating, you start giving away, having a yard sale. But Lila never felt she was growing old, until just a few months ago, when she started getting so tired. When she had babies she never slept. She remembers the years at the factory, when she worked from eight until six and still managed to cook, wash, iron, clean, sew, garden, can, even help with the crops and cows. She never knew when to stop.

When she eloped with Spence, she brought something with her that has lasted to this day—a handful of dried field peas, a special variety that her cousins told her that her mother had raised. Lila kept the peas going in the garden year after year, always saving out some seed. They weren't brown and ordinary. They were white, plumper than most field peas, and she never saw that kind anywhere else. She always called them "our peas."

You grow older, you start reversing direction. Old people draw up in a knot like a baby in the womb. Rosie died curled like a grubworm. Tell Nancy about the peas.

Her mind fights the tranquilizer. She'll fight to the end. I'm stubborn as a Missouri mule, she thinks. I'll accept things up to a point, and then I won't budge.

The way her kids turned out. What will happen to her garden. What they will do with her things. She doesn't care about her things. Junk. She'd rather be outdoors. She never cared about housekeeping.

Playing in her uncle's creek when she was little . . . meeting Spence down in that creek . . . years later when his tractor got stuck in their own creek, hauling him out with the truck. The way he plows her garden lickety-split, clumsily uprooting the precious new slips. She and Spence have spent a lifetime growing things together.

On the wall, the crucifix goes out like a light and there's a strange calm in the corridor, like the hush in church before the preacher begins.

NINETEEN

*I*N THE growing morning light, Spence can hear the airplane coming, a little chug like a hummingbird's surprising motorcycle rumble. He fastened up the calves last night. He hasn't seen Abraham this morning, but Oscar is on the porch with Spence. The tiny single-engine plane flying along the creek line appears so light Spence is sure a good tail wind could make it do a somerset. He watches as Bill flies up and down the largest field, trailing brownish clouds behind him. The wind is from the south, blowing away from the house, so Spence cannot smell the spray. His head is stuffed up from the air-conditioning in the hospital. The plane lifts above the first tree line, barely missing it, then dips down into the second field. At the back, just before reaching the corn, the plane turns and plows back into its own trails of fumes. If Lila dies from that operation and her funeral is Sunday, he could go up in that plane Monday, and if it crashed he would spare Nancy from having to make a separate trip home for his funeral. He had a bad night.

The telephone is ringing. Spence runs inside and grabs the phone, expecting bad news. He has never gotten over the early association between bad news and the telephone.

"Well, how's Lila doing?" a shrill-voiced woman asks. She must be someone Lila knows from her trips with the senior citizens. "They said she was having her neck operated on," the woman continues.

"Yeah. Today—about one o'clock," Spence says, longing for whole minutes of blissful forgetting.

"Lila was looking bad," she says.

You old bat, he thinks, wishing the doctors would saw on *her* neck.

He tells the woman, "Lila's sassing the doctors. Can't nothing hold her down. She's raring to get home and do up her pickles."

"Well, I just wanted to know how she was," the woman says, hanging up abruptly.

It is past seven o'clock. Spence takes a capsule the doctor prescribed for Lila when she had bronchitis back in the winter. The bottle says, "Take one capsule after supper for breathing." The steam from his shaving water helps clear his nose. In the refrigerator, tan beads of glistening moisture dot the sinking meringue of the coconut pie. Nancy and Cat didn't take much of the food. Spence lays four strips of bacon on the bacon rack in the microwave and punches the time buttons. He watches the bacon curl, like time-lapse photography of flowers blooming and dying that he has seen on TV. He stops the oven just before the bell rings. He hates the sound—ping!—like a pebble from a slingshot hitting a hubcap. In the distance, the airplane's engine is receding. Through the window, Spence sees Abraham on the porch licking orange dust from his fur.

After breakfast, he pauses in the doorway of the spare room to look at some of Lila's things—a row of old dolls on a quilt. She bought old dolls at yard sales and cleaned them up and sewed clothes for them. She found a porcelain doll head in the junkhouse behind the barn and made a body for it. Lila can take a scrap of anything and work it into something pretty. The day before, while the girls were freezing the corn, he thought he heard her call him, but it was Cat, and he realized that if Lila died he would hear the girls talking and he would catch an echo of her voice in theirs and think it was her.

*   *   *

At the hospital, she says, "I had a hard night. I didn't sleep a week." She meant wink. She's silly from the drugs. "I'm drunker'n a two-tailed tom," she says, trying to raise her head. After they wheel her away to surgery, Spence strides down the corridor toward the elevator, passing a young woman who says to an older woman, "He wants to get Stevie one of them three-wheelers, but Renée don't want him to have it." A man in a hospital gown trudges down the hall alone, wheeling his I.V. and carrying his piss bag in his hands, carefully, like a baby. The prisoner is out walking too, pressing a folded blanket against his stomach, as if he has had surgery again. He is pale and weak, his eyes buried under those brows that jut out like awnings. He looks half dead.

Downstairs, Spence buys a Coke from the machine and sits at a table by a window in a corner of the cafeteria. Coke always settles his stomach, and the Coke acid helps clean his dentures. The window opens onto a little gray enclosed area—a triangle of grass framed by the angles of the two wings of the building. An updraft suddenly catches some trash and begins spinning it up in the air. A plastic bag and a foil potato-chip bag are dancing and circling, battling each other. As they rise in the updraft, they seem like cartoon characters. They seem alive, a young courting couple chasing and pursuing each other,

[147]

then falling exhausted to the grass before rising up with renewed energy for the chase again. The dance keeps going on for so long Spence sits there, mesmerized.

He loses track of time, and Nancy and Cat find him there.

"Come on, let's eat," says Cat. "When I'm nervous, I have to eat."

Nancy grabs his elbow. "Come on, Dad, they have a lot of food you like. They have corn bread and green beans."

Nancy and Cat travel through the line, knowing exactly what they are doing. Spence hates cafeterias. There are too many choices. As they approach the cashier, he regards with chagrin what he has taken from the salad bar: corn bread, salad with bacon bits, cottage cheese, pineapple, peppers, shredded cheese, cherry tomatoes, dill pickles, crackers.

They sit at a table near the back of the cafeteria, away from the crowd.

"Do you want some of these tommytoes?" he asks Nancy, shoving the cherry tomatoes at her.

"No. I like those fresh tomatoes from Mom's garden. We brought her some the other day, with an onion."

"She saved some of it in a drawer for supper, and you could smell that onion all over the hospital," says Cat with a laugh. "Hey, there's Mom's preacher, Dad."

Spence spots the preacher from Lila's church speaking with a man on the far side of the cafeteria.

"Tell me something, Dad," Nancy says. "I remember the Pentecostals around here never would wear jewelry and makeup. But the PTL Club is Pentecostal, and they decorate themselves like Christmas trees. Why is that?"

"TV commercials," he says.

"I guess so."

"That reminds me. I heard a great joke, Dad," says Cat. "If you scrape off all of Tammy Bakker's makeup, do you know what's underneath?"

"What?"

"Jimmy Hoffa."

Spence can hardly eat. Cat is eating out of nervousness, not missing a bite. Nancy is picking at salad.

"Where do you hear jokes like that, Cat?" asks Nancy. "I never hear jokes."

Cat shrugs. The preacher is headed their way. He stops at their table and lays his hand on Spence's shoulder, saying, "I've got some sick here to look after, but I want you to call me this evening and tell me how she's doing."

"All right," says Spence, cringing. He hates to use the telephone.

The preacher's hand is still on Spence's shoulder, and now the man starts working the muscle. It's supposed to be a friendly and caring gesture, Spence figures, but it makes him nervous. He has never known a man who caressed anybody's shoulder that way. Cat and Nancy are staring at the way the preacher is rubbing on Spence's shoulder.

"I'll be praying real hard for Mrs. Culpepper," the preacher says. He is a young fellow who reminds Spence of the Cards' utility infielder. Spence can't remember the player's name.

TWENTY

ITH HIS CHILDREN, Spence sits in the second-floor waiting room, a small corner area with a Coke machine and a telephone and a TV. The Cards are playing the Astros, and Lee seems absorbed in the game. Nancy is reading a book. Nancy would probably read a book during a nuclear attack. Cat would reach for food, and Lee would go to sleep. Lee always slept when something was bothering him. He would sleep so long it was like a deep illness.

"Dad, what size bra does Mom wear?" asks Cat, who is filling out a form.

"I don't know. Big ones." Five-pound flour sacks.

Nancy says, "When that phone rings, I'm going to jump out of my skin."

Cat folds the form and picks up a women's magazine. A red-white-and-blue Fourth of July cake is on the front. She says to Nancy, "Look at this article, 'How to Warn Your Children About Strangers Without Scaring Them.' I'm at the point where I'm going to have to trust Krystal to know what goes on. I think she's smart. I think she knows what goes on."

In a TV commercial for *Time* magazine, the Pope appears momentarily, holding a strange animal Spence can't identify. "I didn't know the Pope was allowed to have pets," he says.

"He probably needs *some*thing," says Lee, dragging on his cigarette.

A couple about Spence's age enter the waiting area and sit down on a vinyl couch. They stare at the TV. The woman's eyes, with sagging pouches under them, are red from crying. She holds her pocketbook like a lap cat and rubs the material of her skirt nervously. The man, in short sleeves, seems cold. Spence can see the goose pimples on the man's arms.

"Is Joe Magrane pitching today?" the man asks.

"Yeah. He's starting," says Lee, not taking his eyes from the screen.

The man says, "Saint Louis sure goes for those lefties."

"The Cards wouldn't know a right-handed pitcher if he knocked 'em in the head," says Lee.

Jack Clark is up, and he hits a double for the Cards. Spence tries to lose himself in the slow, careful movements of the game. Baseball is the same situations over and over, but no two turn out alike. Like crops and the weather. Life.

When the telephone rings, Cat grabs it. Nancy shuts her book on her thumb and lowers her reading glasses. Spence sees Cat's intake of breath, then her affirmative nod toward them.

"She's O.K.," Cat says, hanging up. "But he thought at first she might have had a slight stroke. When he woke her up, her speech was a little slurred for a minute."

"Her words are always slurred when she's sleepy," Spence says. "That ain't nothing."

"Well, he decided she was all right. He wanted to wake her up as soon as he could, just to see if she had any nerve damage."

"She's O.K. then," Nancy says, breaking into a smile.

"God, I'm relieved!" She holds her book at arm's length. "Look how I'm shaking."

Spence realizes he is shaking too—all the way to his knees.

"Thank God," says Lee. He jams his cap down on his head and turns toward the elevator. "I have to get back to work," he says. "I'll see y'all tonight."

Lila will be in intensive care that night, and they will have to wait until nine o'clock to see her. They will be allowed to see her for fifteen minutes—no more than two persons at a time. Spence decides to go home for a few hours.

In the car, the radio plays "Hearts on Fire" and he sings along with it. Then Phil Collins comes on. Spence can't stand Phil Collins, with his high-pitched yapping, like a pup fastened up in a shed. He turns the radio down. When he drove to the hospital that morning, his head had been full of intolerable imaginings—a funeral in two days. Now his relief empties out his mind, and he drives all the way home as if in a dream.

At home, a loaf of homemade bread wrapped in tinfoil sits on the deck, with a note, "From Hattie Goebel." It is still warm. He stuffs the loaf in a kitchen cabinet, then goes out and cranks up the push mower. He mows the patch around the orchard that he missed a few days before. The mower needs oiling. It keeps sputtering. He's proud of the appearance of his place—well cared for and not trashy. The new siding on the house looks good. After mowing, he reads the newspaper and tries to take a nap, but he can't get to sleep. He gets up and puts on his boots and heads for the back field with a tow sack and a bucket and a shovel.

"Come on, Oscar," he says. "We've got work to do."

For half an hour, he works at transplanting the marijuana plants from the corn row over to the back edge of Bill's land across the creek. He doesn't want to get in trouble with the Frost boys. Maybe Bill thought he was being neighborly, telling Spence about the plants when he might need help with his hospital bills, but it makes Spence angry. He doesn't want a handout. He has never borrowed, and he has always made good on his farm. But the plants in his corn have been bothering him—not the risk, so much. He doubts if the law would find these few plants; they go after major offenders, and he could always claim the seeds strayed from Bill's crop. And it's not that he is being especially virtuous. There's just something about growing them that seems out of character for him. Instead of being an outlaw, he would actually be in fashion, and he never wanted to follow the crowd. It would be like borrowing to buy a combine, or spraying his fields, or getting a credit card, or mortgaging his house—getting in deeper and deeper, like everyone else. He felt helpless when Nancy lectured him about the plastic bottles, but at the moment he feels he can do something. He can imagine the whole farm planted in this stuff someday; it could take over, like jimsonweed and burdock. But not yet.

He waters the plants with buckets of water from the creek. He props a drooping plant against a cornstalk. Oscar, wet and muddy from splashing in the creek, flops down at Spence's feet, spraying water on him.

"Oscar, you sure love to work, don't you, boy?" Spence says, pulling a cocklebur from the dog's shaggy chin.

Spence walks back to the barn in a state of suspension—the worst over but an air of uncertainty remaining, like waiting out a drought.

After feeding the calves, he eats a bowl of cereal and

a piece of baloney and drinks a glass of milk. The news is on. He washes his teeth and runs the dishwasher. He waters the hanging plants on the deck. He feeds Abraham a can of turkey and giblets. Spence dreads calling the preacher.

When he returns to the hospital, Lee is waiting for him in the lounge.

"They moved her to the fourth floor, to the intensive care ward in the heart unit," Lee says.

"What's wrong with her heart?" His own heart somersets.

"Nothing. They just didn't have enough beds in the main unit."

"Oh. You liked to scared me there for a minute."

They crowd into the elevator. There is a hush and a giggle when three more people squeeze in. "The limit's sixteen!" cries a nervous woman in lime-green pants. "Reckon it'll quit on us?" someone asks. Spence squirms. "We've got too many overweight folks in here!" another woman says cheerfully.

In the corridor, Spence asks Lee, "Could you do me a favor and call the preacher?"

"What for?"

"He wanted to know how she was."

"Why can't you call him?"

"He makes me nervous."

The walls of the fourth floor are painted shades of pink, light tones of blood, like blood you spit out when brushing your teeth. As they walk down the hall, Spence says, "Preachers have this act they go into—one for the sick, one for the grief-stricken, one for weddings. They just switch from one to another like they was dialing a TV channel. And then the bull they start in on is like those get-well cards."

"That's their job," says Lee.

Nancy was right. Spence should have taught Lee to farm. If he spent some time out in the fields, he might have a chance to think about things and he wouldn't make so many excuses. Lee's always taking up for the wrong people.

Nancy and Cat are already in the lounge. "She's doing fine," Nancy says. "A nurse just told us she's awake."

Cat's hair is swept up on one side and fastened with an old-fashioned turtle-shell comb. "Did you eat supper?" Cat asks Spence.

"Some cereal and a piece of baloney."

"We went to that new Italian restaurant by the mall," Cat says, making a face at Spence's supper. "It was real good."

"I don't like Italian food," said Spence, wrinkling his nose back at her. "Pizza. Ugh!"

"Heartburn City," says Lee to Spence with a grin.

"We didn't have pizza," says Cat. "We had calamari."

"What's that?"

"Squid," Cat says, eyeing Lee. "I'm surprised I had the nerve to eat it, but I decided to go for it."

The waiting room of the heart unit is large and pleasant, with comfortable chairs and a huge television—a thirty-six-inch, Spence guesses. There is probably more money in heart bypasses than other kinds of surgery, he realizes. People with money probably have more heart trouble because making money is so stressful. The people with stomach problems on the second floor seemed poorer than the people on the fourth floor. A nun slips past the door, almost a hallucination—a penguin. Spence has seen very few nuns, except on TV, but once he saw a nun driving a tractor along a main road, and he puzzled about that for years, inventing histories for her.

He sits there, the music from a rock-and-roll program on TV going through his veins. No one else is watching except him and Cat. If Lila had died during the operation, he thinks now, he would hear rock-and-roll at her funeral. It would be in his head. Lee laughs at him for listening to rock music, but Spence doesn't care. He doesn't really care what people think most of the time. Yet he knows he couldn't have that music at her funeral because of what people would think. If she gets through this illness he might take her dancing again—if his back doesn't act up.

Cat says, "I've got this record. This group is great."

Some long-haired group is swinging bright-colored guitars flamboyantly.

"Their hair looks like they've been rolling around in cow mess," says Spence. Nancy has plunged into her book again, oblivious. "Is your book good?" he asks.

She nods. "Uh-huh."

He should read more, but reading gives him bad headaches. Since he got cable, though, watching TV is an education. When the news shows people in a foreign country, you can tell what the weather is like by what they are wearing. His favorite show is *National Geographic.* He gets to see places he'd never go to—the ocean floor, the North Pole, Siberia, Australia. He loves seeing unusual animals from all over the world. His grandchildren are smart because of all they are exposed to on TV. Sometimes he is flabbergasted by how much they know. They know about dinosaurs, the Japanese yen, satellite communications—the most unlikely subjects.

At nine o'clock a nurse says, "Two of you can go in for ten minutes and then the other two can go in."

"Come on, Lee," Cat says. "Let's you and me go first."

They follow the nurse, and Spence says to Nancy,

"She'll be half asleep, on them tubes. She won't even know they're there."

A moment later he says, "You're right. I should have learnt Lee to farm."

When Nancy and Spence take Cat and Lee's places at nine-fifteen, Lila is awake but too weak to raise her head. She smiles faintly.

"Get out of that bed and rattle them pots and pans!" Spence bellows at her. "We've got to go milk."

"Oh, shoot! I ain't about to get up and go milk," she says. "I've milked enough cows in my time."

She groans and he keeps teasing her, while Nancy places a washrag on Lila's forehead and gives her some water to sip. Her hair is tousled, and she has on no makeup. Tubes are taped to her wrist, and down her neck is the fresh wound, a long slash clamped together with metal staples. The loose flesh under her chin is pulled tight.

Suddenly Cat rushes into the room. "You're missing Mick and Tina!" she says, turning on the small TV that extends from the wall on a long metal neck. She pulls the set toward Lila's bed. "Mick Jagger and Tina Turner!"

"Oh, you don't want to miss Mick and Tina!" Spence says to Lila, clasping her arm.

On the flickering screen, Mick Jagger and Tina Turner are dancing a sexy dance, each singing to the other in a taunting but strangely loving way.

"Look at 'em!" Spence cries, excited by their movements.

"I can't see." As she turns, Lila's tubes dangle before her face. Spence pushes the tubes aside and tilts the TV closer.

"Look at 'em go!" he says gleefully, watching Tina's heavy black body—her big boobs and long legs and wide hips. She's wearing a black leather skirt and fishnet tights. She stomps around in high heels, with her pelvis thrust out. She's like a pickup truck, Spence thinks. Jagger, in contrast, is a lanky beanpole. His big rubbery lips remind Spence of a cow's screw hole.

"Who are they?" says Lila groggily.

"Mick Jagger and Tina Turner," says Nancy.

Spence has a sudden memory—dancing with Cat to Ike and Tina Turner and the Ikettes on the radio. Cat must have been no more than nine.

"How can she be so sexy?" Cat says. "She's no taller than I am and look how wide her hips are."

Tina Turner turns Spence on, the way Lila does—Lila's large, warm, sexy body. Tina is wearing a crazy Halloween fright wig. Her boobs shaking on the screen make him want to cry.

"Hand me that water," Lila says. "I can suck a little ice."

Spence pushes bits of crushed ice between her lips and she crunches it. Then her I.V. unit starts beeping. The fluid isn't getting through the tubes. Nancy fiddles with the tubes, but the machine keeps beeping.

"Where's the nurse?" Spence says impatiently.

Cat goes to look for her. If Lila were a heart patient and the beep signaled danger, she could be dead by now. Intensive care doesn't mean what Spence thought it meant. The nurse ambles in, punches some buttons and jerks the tubes.

"Just two of you are supposed to be in here," she says.

"I'm leaving," Cat says, but her eyes are still stuck to the TV screen.

The amazing thing, Spence realizes now, is that Lila's color has returned. Her face is rosy and full, lighting up every blemish of her complexion, each freckle and age mark and wrinkle. Her face is restored, the way raisins plump up in water.

"Your color looks good," Spence says, holding her hand. She moans a little, a seductive moan, out of place here in the hospital. He is too happy to speak.

He takes the washrag from Nancy and lays it on Lila's forehead. She gazes at the TV. "Who are they?" she says.

And then an incredible thing happens. Mick Jagger grabs Tina Turner's skimpy black leather skirt and rips it off of her and throws it across the stage. There she is in her fishnet tights and black panties, still dancing as if nothing has fazed her. Spence's mouth drops open. "Did you see that?" he says.

"Uh-huh," Lila says. "A colored woman showing her butt." She tries to laugh and her hand goes to her throat, to the ridge of stapled flesh down her neck.

Lila's color looks so good, her face warm and full like a ripe peach. The blood is flowing to her face again. He keeps gazing at her, and she says, "I'll be glad when I get home and don't have everybody staring at me all the time."

Her words sound right. She's not paralyzed. The stuff didn't flow to her brain and damage it.

The nurse reappears, her arm bent so that her watch faces them. "It's been fifteen minutes," she says.

Spence squeezes Lila's hand, and he touches her face. "Your color looks good," he says. The nurse switches off the TV. Mick and Tina have finished their wild dance, and Spence turns to go. "See you tomorrow," he says happily to his wife.

TWENTY-ONE

*T*HE AIRPLANE rumbles and shakes, the propeller whisking the dirt from the airstrip along the edge of Bill's pasture. Spence holds his ears as Bill urges him to climb in. Bill has an oil-stained satchel with him—probably tools to fix the airplane in case it conks out in midair.

"Buckle up, Spence."

"A lot of good that'll do!" yells Spence, fumbling with the seat belt. He's sitting in front, just behind the nose, and Bill is in back, with the dashboard and controls. This is like horse-and-buggy days, with Spence as the horse.

The takeoff reminds Spence of the stock car races at the fairgrounds. Somewhere, Spence heard that certain racing cars were so fast they had to have a parachute in the back to help them brake, and Spence figured it also kept them from taking off into the air.

The airstrip is bumpy with stubble. The plane buck-jumps. "Shake, rattle and roll," Spence sings to himself, feeling a new meaning in that song.

"Here we go!" Bill cries as he points the nose up.

Spence is out of his head to go up with Bill. But it's a joyride. Lila is out of danger, and she will be home on Friday, two days from now. The inspiration came to Spence at 3 A.M. two nights ago. He was dreaming about flying. Enemy planes were spraying the whole ocean with a deadly poison to kill the ships. He was in a Navy fighter, having to decide in a split second whether to live or die.

[161]

In the dream, he was brave, as fearless and determined as those pilots in the war. He woke up, shaking with the horror of it, but he thought if you knew you were going to die, you should soar. It's true, he realized. We know we're going to die—sooner or later. He felt he had to go up in Bill's plane then, to prove he could face the possibility of death as bravely as Lila had. Of course, when Lila hears about this little adventure, she'll kill him.

Up in the air, it's a little smoother. The trees shrink, the fences become lines, the highway a ribbon. A school bus creeps along the highway like an inchworm. Then the airplane dips down and flies lower.

"There's your place, Spence." Bill is shouting, but Spence can barely make out his words above the engine's noise.

They are just above the tree line at the back, where Bill's property joins Spence's farm. To the left is the Frost place. They are flying so low Spence can almost spot the marijuana plants he transplanted into Bill's corn. They cross the line and gain altitude. Spence's farm lies before them. The house squats at the far end. It's pale green with brown shingles. The colors blend into the ground and the grass. The corncrib is barely visible through the woods; the barn sags; the old, unused henhouse seems out of place, parked in the center of the orchard.

All his life, Spence has had a conception of the size and shape and contours of his farm, but whenever he studies the topographical map, it seems somewhat off, not exactly what he knows to be true. Now, above the place, seeing it whole, he realizes it resembles the map after all. The twists and turns of the creek surprise him, though he knows every feature by heart—the little plum tree on a triangular island, the stand of scaly-bark hickory near the crossing, the cluster of birches, the honeysuckle vines that

stay green all winter—all the particulars. But up above, they lose definition and become small parts of something much bigger. His children used to paint pictures by the numbers, and now the farm looks to him like a large design for paint-by-the-numbers. The lone oak tree in the middle field was always so majestic, but now it seems small, a weed. The soybeans are a rich green rug. He is reminded of those giant designs the ancient Indians made in South America. He saw them on a special last year and couldn't get them out of his mind. Those Indians could never have seen their designs whole—big frogs and turtles and cats—yet the outlines were laid out perfectly.

The plane rides rough, but Spence doesn't care. He loves it, the way he used to love riding a cranky mule. Below, the calves are frisking through the pasture, running at the sound of the plane. From up above, they are like puppies playing. Spence smiles. He feels great. Calves playing have always been one of his favorite sights. A surprise for Lila forms in his mind. It's time to stock the pond again. He'll slip some large catfish, two- or three-pounders, in with the little fingerlengths. He wants to see the look on her face when she catches such a big one. She won't expect that. He loves to see her when she's happily surprised. She always laughs so big.

Bill turns the plane and swoops back down over the farm. Spence gazes at his land, his seventy-three acres—cut through by the creek and a stand of trees—and suddenly he sees something new about the layout. The woods are like hair, the two creeks like the parting of a woman's legs, the house and barn her nipples. Spence laughs to himself. He has been sending out a cosmic message to alien explorers and didn't even know it. He wonders if Bill has noticed this configuration—probably not, or he would have pointed it out. Spence wonders if he's losing his mind. Maybe seeing the land that way only means that his mind is on Lila coming home.

At the edge of the upper bean field, Spence notices something else—a tinge of brown. The row of trees at the edge of the field is turning brown. Spence realizes the trees must have been burned by the pesticide. Bill must have flown too low over those trees, or failed to turn off the nozzles when he flew over them, or miscalculated the wind and the distance. The leaves are burnt, the trees endangered. Spence feels sickened, and for a moment he can taste those fumes. He notices the tall oak barked up by lightning in an electrical storm last year. It is dead.

Bill banks the plane and Spence's stomach flips. Then Bill straightens out of the turn and heads toward the largest bean field.

"Hey, Spence!" yells Bill

Spence turns and sees Bill fumbling at the buckles on the satchel he brought. He's not even steering the plane.

"Hey, watch what you're doing!" Spence cries. They're flying over the creek.

But there are no other planes in the air, not even any birds. The plane is up high enough that they won't crash if they hit a bump of air. It feels like driving down an immense, vacant highway—fast and wild because there is nothing to hit. Then from the satchel Bill takes out something familiar—a coffee can. It's that can of seeds. With a grin, Bill snaps the top off the can and pinches some seeds between his finger and thumb. The seeds fly out the window into Spence's soybeans. The first thought that goes through Spence's mind is that he can't strangle Bill here on the spot because they have to get the plane down.

"You crazy idiot!" Spence yells. "You're the one that planted those things in my back field, not the Frost boys!"

"Can't hear you, Spence!" Bill flings out some more

seeds into the field, and the plane zooms on, aiming at some target of its own.

"Stop it. I'll turn you in!"

Cackling with laughter, Bill shouts something Spence can't make out.

Spence yells back, "Well, they won't grow! I'll pull 'em up. You said they need a lot of water." The forecast that morning called for rain. They are due for a good soaking rain, at last. Bill is laughing so much he's paying no attention to flying. They are diving down, heading for the tree line near the barn.

"I'll get you back for this," Spence says. "Set this thing down."

Bill doesn't hear him over the noise of the airplane, but he cuts back on the throttle and the engine seems to stop. He makes a broad swoop just above the trees, then begins turning, heading back, aiming for his airstrip. Below, a herd of Guernseys at the Campbell farm scatters like pieces of a breaking dish.

TWENTY-TWO

"*I*'M REAL PROUD of you for quitting those cigarettes," says Cat as she combs Lila's curls.

"I'm not coughing anymore. I can't get over that." Lila plucks at her blouse, holding the material out on the right side.

"If you do that, people will notice it more," says Cat, slapping at Lila's hand. "Stop it! Don't do that."

"I can't help it. I feel so self conscious."

"You look pretty, Mom," says Nancy, who is gathering up Lila's things.

Lila is in pants and a blouse for the first time in two weeks. She feels warmer with something on her legs. Cat is wearing a wrinkled white cotton dress with a dropped waistline and patch pockets. The dress has threads hanging from the hem and Lila wants to snatch at them.

"That dress needs ironing," she says.

"It's supposed to look wrinkled."

Lila laughs. "All those years I spent ironing. I could have just let y'all go out in wrinkled clothes."

"When you get healed up you can start wearing this." Cat holds up the sample prosthesis that woman left.

"The sandbag," Lila says with a grin. It's still in its plastic envelope, with the pamphlets and letters.

"Here, Nancy, let's don't forget this," says Cat, tossing the package to Nancy. Cat lifts Lila's overnight bag and says, "I'll go get the car and bring it around to the front.

When the nurse gets here to check you out, I guess we'll be ready to go."

Nancy stuffs the package into a paper sack with the water jug, the lotion, the extra Kleenex, all the items that came with the room. She sets the bowl of houseplants from Mattie and Eunice and the basket of artificial violets from Glenda on top of the other things in the sack.

"Do you want to keep these get-well cards, Mom?" she asks.

"Yes. I didn't get to read all the verses."

"People send these cards because they can't think of what to say on their own."

"Well, it's the thought that counts."

But it occurs to Lila how true it is that people either won't or can't come out with their feelings. She appreciates all the cards and the visits from the preacher and the kinfolks and her friends. But there's something wrong, like a wall she's slamming against, like those ocean waves Spence sometimes dreams about. She recalls Rosie clamming up and hiding in herself, for years, where nobody could get to her. Lila married into a family that never knew what to say. Spence is all bottled up and Lee and Nancy are just like him. All those books Nancy reads, and she never has much to say about what she really feels.

Lila says, "You girls sure have been good to me."

"You've been through a lot, Mom," says Nancy, curving her arm around Lila, giving her a tender hug. Lila holds on to Nancy, clutching her close.

"I can't say what I want to say," Lila says. "Maybe I should mail those letters that woman left."

"You don't have to do that, Mom. We understand."

"I never would have thought you all would care this much about me as you've shown," Lila says. "I was always used to doing for y'all, and I never expected you to do for me this way."

"But you deserve it."

It's not words Lila wants. Holding her child is enough, and Nancy is clinging to her, the way Lila once held her baby and read her those meaningless words, those letters from the ocean.

"I guess Spence figured he could get out of coming to the hospital this time," Lila says after Nancy lets go.

"He's busy with a surprise for you," Nancy says, rubbing away a tear. "We offered to come and get you." She glances at her watch. "I'll go find the nurse. This is ridiculous."

It is strange how happy one can be at the worst times. When Spence was on leave from the Navy, before he was sent overseas, Lila felt happy just to be able to see him once more, knowing she might never see him again. Now she feels exhilarated. When the cleaning woman comes in with a cart of equipment and starts talking about her son whose wife suddenly left him, Lila listens eagerly, as if it were the most fascinating story she'd ever heard. The cleaning woman, who is fat, with hair that sprouts out in tufts, says, "His wife left the kitchen in such a mess he had to get me over there to help clean it up! She'd spilled the meat-grease can all over the stove and it was all down in the burners."

The woman begins swabbing the commode with a rag, using her bare hand. Spence would gag if he saw that.

The woman says, "He was in shock. He thought she cared about him, and then she just up and left."

"It can be the other way around too," Lila says happily. "You think your family takes you for granted and then you find out they care a whole lot more than you thought they did."

[169]

"I bet that criminal down the hall don't have no family that's standing behind him," the cleaning woman says.

"Wonder what's wrong with him."

"I heard 'em a-talking and they said he swallowed razor blades, and they went in and didn't get 'em all and had to go back in again."

"Law! And I thought I had troubles!"

"What did they do to you here?" the woman asks, as she swishes her rag in a bucket.

"Oh, I've been through the wringer!" Lila cries. "I've had my tit cut off and my neck gouged out and steeples put in, and I've been stuck with needles all over like a pincushion and put down in cold storage long enough to get pneumonia. And they stole my cigarettes—I ain't had one in two weeks. Did I leave anything out? Oh, and I need new glasses!" Lila pauses to laugh. "I'll be glad when I get out of this place!"

"We sure are going to miss your laugh," a nurse says.

She backs the wheelchair into the room, and Lila sits down. The nurse buckles Lila in, and she feels as if she is in that airplane taking off for Hawaii. As she goes wheeling down the hallway, for some reason she remembers playing ball with the neighbor boys on Sunday afternoons at Uncle Mose's. They liked to pick fights with her, teasing her so much she would beat them up. Her breasts had gone through a short growing season, like something shooting out fast after a long, wet spring. "Been eating sassafras buds, Lila?" they would say, and she would fly into them. She could beat those boys to pieces. She loved that.

TWENTY-THREE

"*I* CAN'T GO TO BED," Lila protests to Spence that afternoon at home. "I don't care how weak I am. I'm sick of laying."

"You've got to build your strength up," Spence says. He didn't go to the hospital that morning because the man was coming to deliver the fish he had ordered. He stocked the pond with fifty fingerlength catfish and twenty-five crappie and an extra twenty-five two-pound catfish, barely finishing before Cat and Nancy got home with Lila. The girls have left but will be back soon. Lila was mad at him for not coming to the hospital to get her. "Was a ball game on?" she accused him. He feels clumsy and nervous with her at home, as if she must be expecting more than just ordinary life now, after her ordeal.

Lila has just discovered the state of the refrigerator and she is ready to clean his plow. "You didn't even touch any of those vegetables I cooked! And I reckon that ham's ruined."

"No, it's not! We eat on it and Lee took some ham and tater salad and half of a cake. And Nancy and Cat eat some when they were here. There was too much grub—we couldn't make away with all of it."

"Who made this coconut pie?"

"I don't remember."

"I love coconut pie better than anything, but that one looks like a tire gone flat."

[171]

She opens the back door and steps onto the deck.

"Where are you going?"

"Out here in the sun. I'm glad I'm back here where I can get warm. I've been cold as a well-digger's butt for two weeks."

"We could go to Florida," he says, following her. "Back to the Everglades."

"No, I ain't never going down there again! That's where I got sick."

"The sun was warm there. It dried out my sinuses and I didn't have any trouble breathing."

"It made me dizzy," she says.

Abraham jumps onto the deck from the milkhouse roof, landing at Lila's feet. He immediately rolls over onto his back, curling his paws and looking at her upside down.

"Well, there's my youngun!" cries Lila, sitting down in the slatted deck chair. "Come here, baby!"

The cat jumps into her lap, purring, and she hugs him. He wriggles away and turns circles in her lap, then jumps down again and rolls over.

"That means he's happy to see me," says Lila proudly. "Did you miss me, Abraham? Law, you've fallen off. You ain't nothing but skin and bones."

"He's been busy," Spence says. "Catching grasshoppers and mice. I see him out in the beans early in the dew, and he comes in looking like a drownded rat."

"He loves them mouses, don't you, Abraham," Lila baby-talks.

The night before, Oscar woke Spence up, barking ferociously at something. From the thrilling sounds of the barks, Spence knew Oscar was excited over an animal, not a human intruder. He wondered if it could be the wildcat.

As he lay awake, he thought with pleasure about the fish he was going to put in the pond. He remembered that the first time he ever laid eyes on Lila was at her uncle's pond. She was fishing. Her bare legs were long, like a crane's. Now he's nervous about his surprise and longs to tell her about it, but he has to save it.

Suddenly Lila is down the steps and striding along the driveway. He has to hurry to catch up with her.

"Where do you think you're going? You're not able to be going out for a hike."

"I'm going to check on the garden," she says, picking up speed. "I just want to see it."

He walks along with her, her legs working fast—her dancing legs. Abraham trots along with them, his tail a bottle brush sticking straight up. Oscar joins them then, scooting out from his dust hole under the car. When Lila arrived from the hospital, they had to hold him to keep him from jumping on her.

"Them vines are firing up," she says.

Despite the recent rain, the garden is drying up in the midsummer heat. Some of the Kentucky Wonder vines have dried up, and the corn is starting to turn brown, but the field peas are thriving among the corn. Lila plunges into the garden, between the okra and the peppers, and leans over to check a pepper.

"That one's ready to pick," she says, snapping it off. She straightens up and twists off a sharp-pointed okra from a stalk. Suddenly Spence realizes she is yanking up weeds and fishing out dirty, stunted cucumbers from beneath dying vines. She snaps off another fuzzy okra, grabs tomatoes.

"Check that corn, Spence. I bet it's hard. It's overgrown, but the field peas look nice."

"What do you think you're doing!" cries Spence. "You ain't got no business out here working in the garden."

"The girls didn't do a thing about those beans like I told 'em to."

"You don't have no gloves on! The doctor said you couldn't handle dirt without gloves. You might get a sore infected and then your arm'll fall off without those lymph nodes."

Lila's hands are full of vegetables, and she cradles them in her left arm. Beads of sweat have popped out on her forehead. She's smiling. "Look at that punkin, would you!" she cries, pointing. "That's going to be the biggest one we ever had! Well, I'll say!" She lets out a big laugh. "That's going to be one for Cinderella!"

Spence stands there, while the sweat on her forehead changes from drops to a moist, smooth layer. Her face is rosy, all the furrows and marks thrusting upward with her smile the way the okra on the stalk reach upward to the sun. Her face is as pretty as freshly plowed ground, and the scar on her neck is like a gully washed out but filling in now. He thinks about the way the soybeans are going to grow those little islands of marijuana, like lacy palm trees waving above the beans, hummocks like those in the Everglades, mounds like breasts. And then he imagines the look on Lila's face when she catches one of those oversized catfish he has slipped into the pond.

"These cucumbers is ready for pickling," Lila says.

"You sure were gone an awful long time," Spence says, his lips puckering up. "I thought to my soul you never *was* going to come home." He takes some of the vegetables from her. "I've got a cucumber that needs pickling," he says.

The way she laughs is the moment he has been waiting for. She rares her head back and laughs steadily, her throat working and her eyes flashing. Her cough catches her finally and slows her down, but her face is dancing like pond water in the rain, all unsettled and stirring with aroused possibility.